序 言

　　「五分鐘學會說英文」第一册出版後，讀者紛紛稱讚這本書的内容靈活，錄音帶精采。内容方面，一個句子可靈活運用到各種場合，而不是學一句只能用在一個地方，因此學起來迅速，效果很好。錄音帶方面，每段實況後唸兩遍英文，一遍中文，也使讀者不受教材限制，隨時隨地都可練習聽講。

　　部分讀者反應錄音帶太過緊湊，中間沒有停頓，使人無法喘口氣，且配合内容的音效如汽車聲、電話鈴聲等不夠多。在此我們要向愛護我們的讀者略作説明。因爲我們錄製的目標就是希望以最少的卷數，包含最多的内容，因此儘量減少非必要的停頓，但也無可避免的犧牲了一些生動的音效。目前「五分鐘學會說英文」第一册四卷錄音帶的長度均已達到極限，恐增加停頓和音效會使卷數增加。

　　「五分鐘學會說英文」第二册的編排方式和第一册相同，每課包括三個實況和「舉一反三」。希望這本書能使您的會話更上一層樓。

編者　謹識

再版的話

　　「五分鐘學會說英文」推出之後，如我們所預期的得到了社會大眾普遍的採用與讚揚。我們了解在工商社會中，大家需要的是一種簡單、易懂、易記而又實用的學習方式。「五分鐘學會說英文」所以能在短時間內銷售一空，正因為有著以上獨特的優點。

　　一位貿易公司的趙經理來信說：五分鐘學英文使得他在與客戶交談時覺得更有自信。榮民總醫院的劉醫師說：「五分鐘學會說英文」使得他出國旅行時有許多現成的句子可用，不必絞盡腦汁去想怎麼講。一位遠在澎湖的王同學來信說這本書使得他學英語的興趣倍增。住在民權西路的徐太太則是一位家庭主婦，她每天聽「五分鐘學會說英文」。她在今年出國探訪兒子，居然也可以說幾句英文，使得全家都很開心。

　　讀者們的來信使我們更有信心再版。書和錄音帶的品質是我們對讀者最大的保證，我們期待著你繼續的批評與指正。

編者　謹識

⏰ *CONTENTS* ⏰

1. Be my guest.

Dialogue 1

A : Is this chair taken? I see a coat on it.
這椅子有人坐嗎？我看到上面有件外套。

B : Oh, that's mine. Let me take it.
哦。那是我的。我來拿走。

A : Are you sure it's all right if I sit here?
你確定我坐在這裡沒有問題嗎？

B : Sure, be my guest.
當然，請便。

A : Well, O.K. then. Thank you.
嗯，那麼，好的，謝謝你。

B : Think nothing of it.
沒什麼。

Dialogue 2

A : I can't find my cigarettes.
我找不到我的香煙。

B : Here, take mine.
喂，拿我的。

A : It's your last one.
這是你最後一根了。

B : It's O.K., be my guest.
沒關係，你用好了。

A : Hey, thanks a lot.
喂，多謝了。

B : You bet.
當然。

Dialogue 3

A : I missed lunch today.
我今天沒吃中飯。

B : Are you hungry? I can cook something for you.
你餓嗎？我可以煮點東西給你吃。

A : I hope I'm not imposing.
我希望我沒打擾到你。

B : No, not at all.
不，一點也不。

A : Well, thanks! I am rather hungry.
嗯，多謝了！我相當餓。

B : Feel free to eat dinner here anytime!
你隨時都可以來這裡吃晚餐！

〔舉一反三〕

A : My I use your pen?
我可以用你的筆嗎？

B : Be my guest.
請便。

A : Do you mind if I use your telephone?
你介意我用你的電話嗎？

B : No, not at all. Be my guest.
不，一點也不。請用。

A : Is this seat taken?
這位子有人坐嗎？

B : No. Be my guest.
沒有。請坐。

A : Could I borrow your car tomorrow evening?
　　我明天晚上可以借你的車子嗎？

B : Certainly. Feel free.
　　當然。隨你用。

A : I hope I'm not imposing on you.
　　我希望我沒打擾到你。

B : No. Feel free to stay here anytime.
　　不會。你隨時都可以留在這裡。

《 背景説明 》

　　Be my guest. 照字面的意思是「我請客。」也就是免費招待對方，讓對方身心都不須負擔。根據這個意思，凡是要表示「請便。」、「別客氣。」，都可用這句話。

　　例如有人跟我們借電話，説： May I use your telephone, please？ 就可用 Be my guest. 回答。別人説 May I sit down？ 或 May I borrow your ball point pen？ 我們也可以用 Be my guest. 回答。

　　Feel free. 「不要拘束。」也可用來代替 Be my guest.

【註釋】

Be my guest. 請便。這句話的意思因使用場合而有所不同，例如説「我請客。」也可用 Be my guest.

think nothing of 認爲無所謂

here 〔hɪr〕 *interj.* 喂（喚人注意之詞）

hey 〔he〕 *interj.* 喂

You bet. 當然。（ = *You can be sure.* ; *Certainly.* ）

impose 〔ɪm'poz〕 *vi.* 打擾；強人所難

2. *First come, first served.*

Dialogue 1

A : They're having a furniture sale at Far Eastern.
遠東公司正在傢俱大減價。

B : Maybe I should go there next week.
或許我下星期該去那裡。

A : No, you have to hurry. It's for one day only.
不，你得趕快。那只有一天。

B : Should we go there tonight, then?
那麼，我們該今晚去嗎？

A : Yes, I think so, because it's first come, first served.
是的，我是這麼想，因為捷足先登。

B : O.K. I'll pick you up after work.
好的。我下班後來接你。

Dialogue 2

A : What are you studying this afternoon?
你今天下午要學什麼？

B : I'm taking a typing class.
我要上打字課。

A : Do you have a typewriter at home to practice on?
你家裡有打字機練習嗎？

B : No, but I can use the typing lab anytime.
沒有，但是我隨時可用打字間。

A : Do you have to reserve a typewriter?

你得先訂打字機嗎？

B : No, it's on a first-come, first-served basis.

不必，那是先去的人先用的。

Dialogue 3

A : Our school is presenting a special concert tonight.

我們學校今晚將演出一場特別的音樂會。

B : Oh really? What sort of concert?

真的啊？哪種音樂會？

A : It'll be folk music from different countries.

是來自各國的民謠。

B : I'd like to come. Do I need to make reservations?

我想去。我要先訂位嗎？

A : No, it's first come, first seated.

不用，那是先到先坐的。

B : What time is it? I should go early.

幾點鐘？我該早點去。

〔舉一反三〕

A : Should we go to the big sale today?

我們今天要去大拍賣嗎？

B : Yes, we'll have to go early. It's first come, first served.

是的，我們得早點去。捷足先登。

A : I heard they're giving away free tickets for the theater.

我聽說他們在送免費戲票。

B : Yes, let's hurry. It's first come, first served.

是的，我們趕快。先到先得。

A : Do we have to reserve a tape recorder in the language lab?
　　我們得預訂語言教室的錄音機嗎?

B : No, it's on a first-come, first-served basis.
　　不用,那是先到先用的。

A : Should we make reservations for the play?
　　我們要預訂這話劇的座位嗎?

B : No, it's first come, first seated.
　　不用,那是先到先坐的。

A : Isn't there a sale on suits at Shin Kong?
　　新光公司不是有套裝大減價嗎?

B : Yes, suits are half price for one day only.
　　是的,套裝只這一天半價。

【註釋】

First come, first served. 先到先得;捷足先登。

lab〔læb〕*n.* 實驗室;研究室

give away 贈送

the theater 戲劇;戲劇表演

recorder〔rɪˈkɔrdɚ〕*n.* 錄音機

3. *Can you save my place, please?*

Dialogue 1

A : Excuse me. Do you have the time?
　　對不起。你知道幾點嗎？

B : Yes. It's 10 : 45.
　　知道。現在是十點四十五分。

A : Oh, no, I've got to make a phone call. Can you save my place, please?
　　哦，不。我得打電話。請你幫我留位置好嗎？

B : Sure. Go ahead.
　　好的，去吧。

A : I should be back in a few minutes.
　　我過幾分鐘就回來。

B : No problem.
　　沒問題。

Dialogue 2

A : Oh, dear!
　　噢，老天！

B : What's the matter?
　　怎麼了？

A : I'm afraid I've left my purse in my car!
　　我恐怕把錢包放在汽車裡了！

B : Well, you'd better go and get it before you buy your ticket.
　　那麼你最好在買票前去拿來。

A : Could you save my place in line, please?
　　請你幫我排隊留位置好嗎?

B : Yes, of course. Hurry up!
　　好,當然好。趕快!

Dialogue 3

A : Excuse me. Are you in line?
　　對不起。你在排隊嗎?

B : No, I'm not. The line starts over there.
　　不,我沒在排隊。隊伍從那裡開始。

A : Has it been moving?
　　它在動嗎?

B : Yes, I think it's moving pretty fast.
　　是的,我想它動得很快。

A : I'd better get in line right now.
　　我最好馬上就排隊。

B : Yes, I guess you should.
　　是的,我想你應該這樣。

〔舉一反三〕

A : Could you save my place, please?
　　請你幫我留位置好嗎?

B : Certainly, go ahead.
　　當然,去吧。

A : Can you save my place in line? I have to get something.
　　你幫我排隊留位置好嗎?我得去拿一樣東西。

B : O.K. But don't take too long.
　　好的,但是不要太久。

A : Excuse me. Is this the line for the cafeteria?

對不起。這隊伍是排到自助餐廳的嗎?

B : Yes, it is.

是的,它是。

A : Can I have a hamburger and some coffee?

給我一份漢堡和咖啡好嗎?

B : I'm sorry, you'll have to get in line.

抱歉,你得排隊。

A : Can you save my place? I have to go outside.

你能不能幫我留個位置?我得到外面去。

B : Yes, but please hurry.

好的,但請快點。

【註釋】

Do you have the time? 你知道現在幾點嗎?

Do you have time? 你有空嗎?

cafeteria (‚kæfə'tırıə) *n.* 自助餐廳

Yes, of course. Hurry up!

Could you save my place in line, please?

4. Can you keep an eye on my bag?

Dialogue 1

A : Excuse me, sir. 對不起，先生。

B : What can I do for you?
要我為你做什麼嗎？

A : Can you keep an eye on my bag?
請你幫我看管我的袋子好嗎？

B : Certainly. Will you be gone long?
好的。你會去很久嗎？

A : No, I just have to make a phone call.
不會，我只要去打個電話。

B : Go ahead. It'll be safe with me.
去吧。我會好好保管你的袋子。

Dialogue 2

A : Where's my jacket?
我的夾克在哪裡？

B : I don't know. Where did you leave it?
我不知道。你把它放在哪裡？

A : I just put it on this chair and now it's gone.
我剛才就放在這張椅子上，現在卻不見了。

B : Are you sure? 你確定嗎？

A : Of course I'm sure! I bet somebody stole it.
我當然確定！我敢打賭一定是被偷了。

B : You should have kept an eye on it.
你本該注意的。

Dialogue 3

A : Oh, dear! I forgot my dental appointment.
天啊！我忘了去看牙齒。

B : When was it for?
原來定在幾點？

A : It was for 10 o'clock this morning.
定在今天早上十點。

B : It looks like you'll have to make another appointment.
看來你得再約一次了。

A : I know. Now the dentist will be mad at me.
我知道。現在牙醫師會生我的氣。

B : You ought to keep track of your appointments more carefully.
你該更小心注意你的約定。

〔舉一反三〕

A : Can you keep an eye on my coat?
請你幫我看管我的大衣好嗎？

B : Sure, I'll be glad to.
好的，我很樂意這麼做。

A : Did anyone take my seat?
有人坐了我的位子嗎？

B : No, I kept an eye on it.
沒有，我看著它。

A : I keep track of my expenses in a notebook.
我在筆記上記我的開銷。

B : That's a good idea.
那是個好主意。

A : Did you make an appointment with your doctor?
你和你的醫生約好看病的時間嗎?

B : No, I forgot all about it.
不,我忘得一乾二淨了。

A : I can't find my wallet anywhere.
我到處都找不到我的錢包。

B : I bet it's in your pocket.
我打賭在你的口袋裡。

《背景說明》

要請別人幫忙照顧一下行李、衣物等時,不可用 *Can you see my ~?* 要用 *Can you keep an eye on my ~?*

要注意 *keep an eye on* 這個成語照字面容易誤解為「睜一隻眼,閉一隻眼」,實際上是「注意;照顧」的意思。因此要去買票而託夥伴照顧行李,可以說 *Keep an eye on* my suitcase while I buy my ticket. 出遠門託鄰居注意門戶,也可說:*Can you keep an eye on* my house while I'm away?

【註釋】

keep an eye on 看管;留意;注意
I bet. 我有把握;我敢打賭;我確信。
should have + p.p. 表過去該做而未做的事
dental 〔'dɛntḷ〕 *adj.* 牙齒的;齒科的
be mad at 生~的氣
keep track of 非常注意;記住
expense 〔ɪk'spɛns〕 *n.* 消費

5. Let's keep in touch.

Dialogue 1

A : I hear you're moving to Kaohsiung.
　　我聽說你要搬到高雄。

B : Yes, I found a very good job down there.
　　是的，我在那裡找到一份很好的工作。

A : Well, we'll certainly miss you in Taipei.
　　嗯，我們在台北一定會想念你的。

B : I'm going to miss you folks, too.
　　我也會想念你們。

A : Let's keep in touch.
　　讓我們保持聯繫。

B : O.K. I'll drop you a line as soon as I get there.
　　好的。我一到那裡就會給你寫信。

Dialogue 2

A : How long have you been living in Chicago?
　　你在芝加哥住了多久？

B : Oh, about four years now.
　　到現在大約四年了。

A : Where do your parents live?
　　你父母住在哪裡？

B : They still live in Taipei where I was born.
　　他們仍然住在我的出生地台北。

A : Do you write or call them very much?
　　你常寫信或打電話給他們嗎？

B : Yes, I try to keep in touch with them.
　　是的，我試著和他們保持聯繫。

Dialogue 3

A : I just got a letter from an old high school buddy.
我剛接到一封高中老朋友的信。

B : Really? That's nice.
眞的？那眞好。

A : He usually keeps me posted.
他常寫信給我。

B : I've been completely out of touch with my old friends.
我和我的老朋友已完全失去聯繫。

A : It's hard to keep up contact when people move around so much.
大家經常搬家，很難保持聯絡。

B : Yes, people just seem to drift apart.
是的，大家似乎疏遠了。

〔舉一反三〕

A : I'll be leaving for New York tomorrow.
我明天要去紐約了。

B : Let's keep in touch.
讓我們保持聯繫。

A : Is Bob an old friend of yours?
鮑伯是你的老朋友嗎？

B : Yes. We've kept in touch for many years.
是的。我們多年來一直保持聯繫。

A : Is this postcard from your brother in Mexico?
這明信片是你在墨西哥的哥哥寄來的嗎？

B : Yes, he keeps me posted regularly.
是的，他定期給我寫信。

A : All right, Mr. Jones. We hope to hear from you
during your trip.

好的，瓊斯先生。我們希望在你旅途中接到你的信。

B : Yes, sir. I'll be sure to keep you informed.

好的。我一定會和你聯絡的。

A : Have you heard from Jean Stafford lately?

你最近有沒有接到琴・史丹福的信？

B : No, we've been out of touch for almost a year.

沒有，我們將近一年來都沒有聯繫。

【註釋】

keep in touch 保持聯繫
drop sb. a line 寄給某人一封短信
buddy (ˈbʌdɪ) n. 〔美口〕夥伴；老兄（對熟朋友的稱呼）
keep sb. posted 寫信給某人
keep up 保持
drift apart 疏遠

Let's keep in touch.

I'll be leaving for New York tomorrow.

6. *I don't have the vaguest idea.*

Dialogue 1

A : Did you see Jane today?
你今天看到珍了嗎？

B : Yes, why does she have such a long face?
看到了，她爲什麼拉長了臉？

A : I don't have the vaguest idea.
我一無所知。

B : I would have thought she'd be happy.
我以爲她該高興的。

A : Especially since she got her promotion.
尤其因爲她升了。

B : Maybe it's some personal problem.
或許是個人的問題吧。

Dialogue 2

A : Listen to my car. It's making a strange noise.
聽聽我的車子，有個很奇怪的聲音。

B : Yes, you're right. That sounds pretty bad.
是的，你對了。那聽起來很糟糕。

A : Well, what's wrong with it?
它有什麼毛病？

B : I don't have the vaguest idea.
我一點概念也沒有。

A : I thought you knew all about cars.
我以爲你對汽車無所不知。

B : Not really. All I know is how to change a flat tire.
並非如此。我所知道的只是如何換洩了氣的輪胎。

Dialogue 3

A : Has Bob moved yet?
　　鮑伯已經搬了嗎？

B : Yes, he moved out last weekend.
　　是的，他上週末搬出去的。

A : I wonder if he's paying more for rent now.
　　不知道現在他是否付更多的房租。

B : I don't have the faintest idea.
　　我一點都不知道。

A : Anyway, he's probably glad to leave that noisy building.
　　無論如何，他或許高興離開那棟吵鬧的房子。

B : Yes, he is. I know that for sure.
　　是的，他是很高興。我確知如此。

〔舉一反三〕

A : Do you think Bob is happily married?
　　你認為鮑伯結婚結得高興嗎？

B : I don't have the vaguest idea.
　　我一點都不知道。

A : Can you fix my television?
　　你能修我的電視機嗎？

B : I don't have the vaguest idea how to fix it.
　　我一點都不知道怎麼修。

A : I wonder how much money Mary makes.
　　不知道瑪莉賺多少錢。

B : I don't have the slightest idea.
　　我一點也不知道。

A : Is it going to rain tomorrow?
　　明天會下雨嗎？

B : I don't have the faintest idea.
　　我一點都不知道。

A : Jim doesn't know much about cars.
　　吉姆對汽車懂得不多。

B : No, he doesn't have the slightest idea.
　　不，他一點都不懂。

【註釋】

have a long face 拉長臉

vague〔veg〕*adj.* 模糊的；不清楚的（＝*faint*）

would have＋p.p. 表與過去事實相反的假設

flat tire 洩了氣的輪胎

for sure 確定地（＝*for certain*）

I don't have the vaguest idea.

7. *Do you have change for a dollar?*

Dialogue 1

A : Do you have change for a dollar?
　　你有沒有可以換一塊錢的零錢？

B : I think so. Why?
　　我想有的。什麼事？

A : I need some change for the bus.
　　我需要一些坐公車的零錢。

B : How do you want it?
　　你要怎樣的？

A : I need a couple of quarters and five dimes.
　　我需要兩個二角五分，和五個一角的。

B : Here you are.
　　這就是。

Dialogue 2

A : Do you want to take some time for coffee?
　　你要不要花點時間喝咖啡？

B : Sure. There's a coffee machine around the corner.
　　當然。轉角處有一台咖啡機。

A : Wait a minute. How much is the coffee?
　　等一下。這咖啡要多少錢？

B : It's 20 ¢ a cup.
　　一杯要兩角。

A : All I have is a quarter, and the machine says "EXACT CHANGE."

我只有二角五分的，而這機器上說要「確實數目」的零錢。

B : That's O.K. I have change for your quarter.

沒關係。我有零錢可換你的二角五分。

Dialogue 3

A : Excuse me, Ma'am.

對不起，女士。

B : Yes, can I help you?

是的，我能為你服務嗎？

A : Yes, I need to change a dollar for the parking meter.

是的，我需要換一塊錢，放到停車計時表裡。

B : I'm sorry. We're not allowed to give change.

抱歉，我們不准給零錢。

A : Oh, all right. I'll buy a candy bar.

沒關係。我買一塊糖。

B : Certainly, sir. Here's your change.

好的，先生。這是你的零錢。

〔舉一反三〕

A : Do you have change for a dollar?

你有沒有可以換一塊錢的零錢？

B : Yes, I have four quarters.

有的，我有四個二角五分。

A : Will you take the bus?

你要坐公車嗎？

B : I will if I can get change for a dollar.

如果我能把一塊錢換成零錢就坐。

A : Let's go play some pinball.
　　我們去打彈球吧。

B : O.K., I have lots of change.
　　好的。我有很多零錢。

A : Do you have change for a dollar?
　　你有可以換一塊錢的零錢嗎？

B : Yes, but I need it to do my laundry.
　　有，但是我要用來洗衣服。

A : Where can I change a dollar?
　　我可以到哪裏去換一塊錢？

B : There's a bank right down the street.
　　沿街走下去有家銀行。

【註釋】

change〔tʃendʒ〕*n.* 零錢

quarter〔'kwɔrtɚ〕*n.*〔美〕二角五分

dime〔daɪm〕*n.*〔美〕一角

Ma'am〔mæm , mɑm〕*n.*〔俗〕女士；夫人（ = *madam* ）

meter〔'mitɚ〕*n.* 計量器

candy bar 單獨包裝的塊狀糖

pinball〔'pɪn,bɔl〕*n.* 彈球遊戲

laundry〔'lɔndrɪ , 'lan-〕*n.* 要洗的衣服

do one's laundry 洗衣服

8. *That's a steal.*

Dialogue 1

A : Did you see the ads for color TVs at Ward's?
你有沒有看到瓦茲店彩色電視機的廣告？

B : No. Are they on sale?
有。它們是減價的嗎？

A : I'll say! They have 19-inch portables for $149.
是的！他們十九吋手提電視機賣一百四十九元。

B : Wow! That's a steal.
哇！那眞便宜。

A : They also have a good deal on dishwashers.
他們的洗碗機也賣得很便宜。

B : I should look into that.
我要研究一下。

Dialogue 2

A : Do you like my jacket?
你喜歡我的夾克嗎？

B : It's beautiful. Was it expensive?
很好看。它貴嗎？

A : No, it was a real steal.
不，它眞便宜。

B : Was it on sale? 它是減價品嗎？

A : No. I get a big discount at the clothing store where
I work. 不是。我在我工作的地方買的，有大折扣。

B : That's alright. You're lucky.
那眞好。你很幸運。

Dialogue 3

A : Do you want anything from the grocery store?
　　你要不要從雜貨店買點什麼？

B : Yes, pick up a gallon of milk.
　　好的，買一加侖牛奶。

A : How much will it cost?
　　要多少錢？

B : Only $1.39 this week.
　　這週只要一塊三毛九。

A : That's a steal! It must be on sale.
　　那真便宜！一定是在減價。

B : Yes, that price should bring in plenty of customers.
　　是的，那種價錢該會招來許多顧客。

〔舉一反三〕

A : A gold watch! When did you get rich?
　　一隻金錶！你什麼時候發財的？

B : I didn't. I got a good deal.
　　我沒有。我撿了個便宜。

A : At that price, it's a steal.
　　賣那個價錢實在太便宜了。

B : At that price you'd better see if it works, first.
　　賣那個價錢，你最好先看看能不能用。

A : I was hoping to get a bargain.
　　我以為撿了便宜貨。

B : Next time, look for quality and not just a steal.
　　下次注意品質，不要只想買便宜的。

A : Didn't James get a good deal on his car?
　　詹姆士的車子不是買得很便宜嗎？

B : Yes, I think he got 20 percent off.
　　是的，我想他是用八折價買的。

A : I bought this couch for half price.
　　我用半價買了這長沙發。

B : That's quite a bargain.
　　買得真便宜。

【註釋】

ads 為 advertisements 的縮寫，意為「廣告」。

I'll say. 是的；一點也不錯。

portable〔'portəbḷ, 'por-〕*n.* 可手提的東西

wow〔waʊ〕*interj.* 哇

steal〔stil〕*n.* 很便宜買到的東西

dishwasher〔'dɪʃ,wɑʃɚ〕*n.* 洗碗機

look into 研究；調查

discount〔'dɪskaʊnt〕*n.* 折扣

alright〔ɔl'raɪt〕*adv.* = *all right*

grocery〔'grosɚɪ〕*n.* 食品雜貨

pick up 攜帶

couch〔kaʊtʃ〕*n.* 長沙發

9. *Let's call it a day.*

Dialogue 1

A : This was a very good meeting, Al.
艾爾，這次會議很棒。

B : Thanks. I hope we cleared up some problems.
謝謝。我希望我們解決了一些問題。

A : I think we did. Is there anything else to discuss?
我想我們解決了。還有什麼要討論的？

B : No, that's all.
沒有，就那些了。

A : Then, let's call it a day.
那麼，我們今天到此為止。

B : All right. See you tomorrow.
好的。明天見。

Dialogue 2

A : Did we finish packing all the orders?
所有的訂貨我們都包裝完了嗎？

B : No, we still have to do about ten more.
沒有，我們大約還有十件。

A : I'm tired of packing this stuff.
我厭倦了包裝這東西。

B : Maybe we could finish it later.
或許我們可以以後做。

A : Sure, we could do it first thing tomorrow morning.
當然，我們可以明早一來就做。

B : O.K. Let's call it a day.
好的。我們今天到此為止。

Dialogue 3

A : What a week!
多累的一週！

B : Really! I've never seen so much work.
眞的！我從沒看過這麼多工作。

A : I'm so happy just to go home.
我只要回家就很高興了。

B : Right. T.G.I.F!
對。感謝上帝，禮拜五了。

A : Well, have a nice weekend.
嗯，週末愉快。

B : Thank you. You, too!
謝謝你。週末愉快。

〔舉一反三〕

A : Is everything finished?
都做完了嗎？

B : I think so. Let's call it a day.
我想是的。我們今天到此爲止。

A : I'm really too tired to work anymore.
我眞的太累了，不能再工作了。

B : O.K. Let's call it a day.
好的。我們今天到此爲止。

A : Let's call it a day and go home.
我們今天到此爲止，回家吧。

B : I'm afraid we can't. We still have some more
work to do.
我恐怕我們沒辦法。我們還有一些工作要做。

A : Well, the week's over, and today is payday.
這週結束了，今天是發薪的日子。

B : T.G.I.F.!
感謝上帝，禮拜五了。

A : Have a nice weekend. I'll see you Monday.
週末愉快。星期一見。

B : The same to you. Goodbye!
你也一樣。再見！

【註釋】

clear up 解決

call it a day 今天到此為止

order〔'ɔrdɚ〕*n.* 訂貨

be tired of 對～厭倦

stuff〔stʌf〕*n.* 東西

first thing 首先；立刻

T.G.I.F! 感謝上帝，禮拜五了。原句是 Thank God it's Friday!

10. I'm being helped.

Dialogue 1

A : That's a beautiful skirt you're wearing.
　　妳穿的裙子很漂亮。

B : Thank you. I bought it in Mexico.
　　謝謝你。我在墨西哥買的。

A : Could I show you some blouses in a matching color?
　　要我給妳看些顏色相配的短上衣嗎?

B : No, thank you. I'm being helped.
　　不用,謝謝你。已經有人為我服務了。

A : Well. I hope you find something you like.
　　那麼我希望你找到你喜歡的東西。

B : I hope so, too.
　　我也希望如此。

Dialogue 2

A : May I help you?
　　我能為你服務嗎?

B : Yes. Do you have these shoes in size 7 1/2?
　　是的。你這鞋子有沒有七號半的?

A : I'm not sure. They may be out of stock.
　　我不確定。它們可能正缺貨。

B : I'd like to try on a pair if you have them.
　　如果你有的話,我想試穿一下。

A： I'll look in the stockroom.
　　我去儲藏室看一下。

B： If you don't have these shoes, I'll try a similar style.
　　如果你沒有這種鞋子，我會試樣子差不多的。

Dialogue 3

A： Are you being helped?
　　有人招呼你嗎？

B： No, I'm not. I'm interested in some scarves.
　　不，沒有。我想看些圍巾。

A： All our scarves are in this section.
　　我們所有的圍巾都在這區。

B： I'm really just looking for something warm.
　　我真的只想找件溫暖的東西。

A： Well, maybe you'd like a heavy wool scarf.
　　那麼，或許你要一條厚的羊毛圍巾。

B： Yes, that's what I want.
　　是的，那正是我要的。

〔舉一反三〕

A： Can I show you something?
　　要我給你看些什麼？

B： No, thanks. I'm already being helped.
　　不用了，謝謝。已經有人為我服務了。

A： Are you being helped?
　　有人招呼你嗎？

B： No, I'm not. I'd like to see some overcoats.
　　不，沒有。我想看些大衣。

A : May I help you?
　　我能為你服務嗎？。

B : No, I'm just looking.
　　不用，我只是看看。

A : Are you being waited on?
　　有人為你服務嗎？

B : No, I'd like to have some coffee.
　　沒有，我想來點咖啡。

A : Have you been served?
　　有人為你們服務嗎？

B : No, we'd like to order now.
　　沒有，我們現在要點東西。

【註釋】

blouse〔blauz〕*n.* 女用短上衣

out of stock 缺貨

stockroom〔'stɑk,rum〕*n.* 儲藏室

scarf〔skɑrf〕*n.* 圍巾

wait on 侍候

11. I couldn't help it.

Dialogue 1

A : What was that terrible noise?
　　那可怕的噪音是什麼？

B : I dropped a stack of dishes.
　　我打翻了一堆盤子。

A : Why did you drop the dishes?
　　你爲什麼打翻盤子？

B : I couldn't help it. They were slippery.
　　我沒辦法。它們很滑。

A : Well, try to be more careful next time.
　　好吧，下次試著更小心點。

B : Yes, sir. I sure will.
　　是的，先生。我一定會的。

Dialogue 2

A : You didn't show up for dinner last night.
　　你昨晚沒來吃飯。

B : I know, I'm awfully sorry.
　　我知道，我非常抱歉。

A : Why didn't you let me know you weren't coming?
　　你爲什麼不讓我知道你不來呢？

B : I couldn't help it. My mother was in a car accident.
　　我沒辦法。我媽媽出車禍了。

A : Oh, that's terrible. Is she O.K.?
　　哦，那眞糟糕。她還好嗎？

B : She wasn't hurt, but she was badly shaken up.
　　她沒受傷，但是她被震動得厲害。

Dialogue 3

A : I'm upset. Somebody told my boss I have a part-time job.

我很難過。有人告訴我的老板，我在兼差。

B : And he doesn't like that ?

他不喜歡你兼差嗎？

A : No, he doesn't. He thinks I'm too tired to work.

不，他不喜歡。他認為我太累了，沒辦法工作。

B : I'm sorry. I have to admit I told him.

抱歉。我得承認是我告訴他的。

A : You told him ? Why ?

你告訴他的？為什麼？

B : I couldn't help it. He asked me point-blank.

我沒辦法。他直截了當地問我。

〔舉一反三〕

A : You missed class yesterday.

你昨天沒來上課。

B : I couldn't help it. I was at the dentist.

我沒辦法。我去看牙醫了。

A : You're late again !

你又遲到了！

B : I couldn't help it. My alarm didn't go off.

我沒辦法。我的鬧鐘沒響。

A : Did you eat all the cookies ?

你把所有的餅乾都吃掉了嗎？

B : I couldn't help myself. They were so good.

我沒辦法。它們太好吃了。

A : You aren't very alert today.

　　你今天不太細心。

B : I can't help it. I couldn't sleep last night.

　　我沒辦法。我昨晚睡不好。

A : You look very nice today.

　　你今天看起來很漂亮。

B : I can't help it. I was born beautiful.

　　沒辦法,我生來就漂亮。

─────────────────────────────────

【註釋】

　　stack〔stæk〕*n.* 大量;堆

　　slippery〔'slɪpərɪ〕*adj.* 滑的

　　show up 出現

　　point-blank〔'pɔɪnt'blæŋk〕*adj.* 率直的

　　go off (鬧鐘)響

　　alert〔ə'lɜt〕*adj.* 留心的

12. *Something's come up.*

Dialogue 1

A : Bob, are you going to show up at the meeting?
鮑伯，你今晚要去開會嗎？

B : No, I can't make it tonight. Something's come up.
不去，我今晚沒辦法去。有點事。

A : Are you sure you can't make it? This meeting is very important.
你確定你沒辦法去嗎？這會議很重要。

B : I know, but I really can't. It's a family problem.
我知道，但是我眞的沒辦法。這是個家庭問題。

A : Well, O.K. I'll tell you about the meeting tomorrow.
嗯，好吧。我明天會告訴你這個會全講些什麼。

B : Thanks. I'm sure I'll make the next meeting.
謝謝。我相信我下次一定能去。

Dialogue 2

A : Can you go with us to the basketball game Thursday?
你星期四能和我們一起去看籃球賽嗎？

B : No, I'm afraid not.
不行，我恐怕不能去。

A : I thought you wanted to see Boston play.
我以爲你想看波士頓打。

B : I do very much, but something's come up.
我是很想看，但是有事。

A : Nothing serious, I hope.

　　我希望不是什麼嚴重的事。

B : No, but I really have to do something else.

　　不是，但是我得做其他的事。

Dialogue 3

A : Why wasn't Judy at work today?

　　茱蒂今天為什麼沒來上班？

B : Apparently, something came up and she couldn't come.

　　很明顯地，發生了什麼事，所以她沒辦法來。

A : I wonder what happened?

　　不知道發生了什麼事？

B : I think it's her little boy. He's been pretty sick.

　　我想是她的小男孩。他一直病得很重。

A : Did she take him to the hospital?

　　她帶他去醫院了嗎？

B : I don't know. I'm only guessing.

　　我不知道。我只是猜猜而已。

〔舉一反三〕

A : Are you going with us to the movies tonight?

　　你今晚要和我們一起去看電影嗎？

B : No, I'm sorry. Something's come up.

　　抱歉我不去。有事。

A : Weren't you at the party last night?

　　你昨晚沒去舞會？

B : No, I couldn't come. Something's come up.

　　沒有，我沒辦法去。發生了一些事。

A : I'm sorry I can't make it. Something unexpected has come up.

抱歉我沒辦法。發生了一些意外。

B : Oh, I hope it isn't serious.

我希望不嚴重。

A : We're having some friends for dinner. Can you make it?

我們要請一些朋友來吃晚飯，你能不能來？

B : I think so. Let me call my wife.

我想可以。讓我打個電話給我太太。

A : What time should I pick you up?

我該什麼時候來接你？

B : Let me think. Can you make it at 6 o'clock?

我想想。你能六點來嗎？

【註釋】

come up 出現

13. I goofed up.

Dialogue 1

A : I'm sorry, but I didn't finish mailing those letters.
抱歉，我沒寄完那些信。

B : What happened? 發生了什麼事？

A : Oh, I goofed up the zip codes.
我把郵遞區號弄錯了。

B : How could you do that?
你怎麼會弄錯？

A : Well, I wrote Illinois zip codes on the out-of-state addresses.
嗯，我把伊利諾的郵遞區號，寫在別州的地址上。

B : You'll have to address them over again.
你得重寫地址了。

Dialogue 2

A : Hey, Jerry, what did you do with the Acme order?
嗨，傑瑞，艾克明的訂貨，你怎麼處置了？

B : The Acme order? I mailed it out this morning.
艾克明的訂貨嗎？我今天早上寄出去了。

A : Oh, no! That order wasn't complete.
哦，不！那訂貨還沒弄好。

B : I guess I goofed up.
我想我弄錯了。

A : You sure did. You should have read the invoice.
我當然弄錯了。你應該看發貨單的。

B : Now I'll have to send a second package.
現在我得再送一個包裹。

Dialogue 3

A : How is your house-painting coming along?
你家裡的油漆進行得怎樣？

B : Not so good. I messed it up.
不怎麼好。我弄得亂七八糟。

A : How did you do that?
怎麼弄的？

B : I used the wrong kind of paint.
我用錯了漆。

A : You have to be careful about that.
你得小心。

B : Right. Now I have to do it all over again.
是的。現在我得重新來過。

〔舉一反三〕

A : Did you finish fixing your car?
你的車子修好了嗎？

B : No, I goofed it up.
不，我弄錯了。

A : I messed up that order for the Acme Company.
我把艾克明公司的訂貨弄亂了。

B : Now you'll have to do it over again.
現在你得重做。

A : How is your garden coming along?
你的花園進行得怎樣？

B : It's coming along very well.
進行得很好。

A : Do I have to do my homework over again?
　　我的家庭作業得重做嗎？
B : No, I don't think so.
　　不，我想不必。

A : What's wrong with your television?
　　你的電視有什麼毛病？
B : The picture is all goofed up.
　　畫面很亂。

《背景說明》

　　goof up 是常用的俚語，表示「弄錯；弄亂」，可代替 make a mistake 和 mess up。譬如有人問你 How was your English exam?如果考得不好，可以說：*I goofed it up*.

　　由於 goof 這個字當名詞時，表示「傻瓜；呆子」，因此 *goof up* 本身就有「因缺乏智識而造成」的含意，make a mistake 和 mess up 可能是因疏忽所造成的，兩者稍有不同。

【註釋】

goof up 犯錯
zip code （美國的）郵遞區號
do with 處置
order (ˋɔrdɚ) *n.* 訂貨
should have＋**p.p.** 表過去該做而未做的事
invoice (ˋɪnvɔɪs) *n.* 發貨單

14. Let's get to the point.

Dialogue 1

A : Mr. Brown, do you feel I've done a good job for the company?

布朗先生，你認爲我做的對公司有益嗎？

B : Of course, Mr. Yi. You're a valuable employee.

當然，易先生。你是個很有價值的雇員。

A : I'm glad you think so. I enjoy working here.

我很高興你這麼想。我喜歡在這裡工作。

B : Let's get to the point, Mr. Yi. Is there something on your mind?

讓我們來談要點，易先生。你有心事嗎？

A : Yes, Mr. Brown.

是的，布朗先生。

B : Then let's hear it.

那麼我們來聽聽。

Dialogue 2

A : Good afternoon, Bob. Isn't it a lovely day?

午安，鮑伯。這不是個可愛的日子嗎？

B : Yes, it is, Janet.

是的，珍妮特。

A : It's the kind of day when you want to go outside.

這就是那種使你想出去的日子。

B : Janet, let's get to the point. Do you want the afternoon off?

珍妮特，我們來談要點。妳今天下午想休息嗎？

A : Yes, Bob!

　　是的，鮑伯！

B : Alright. As soon as you finish typing, you can go.

　　好的。妳一打完字，就可以走。

Dialogue 3

A : I don't think I can afford to buy your car.

　　我認為我買不起你的車子。

B : But it's in perfect condition. It's almost new.

　　但是這車子狀況非常好。它幾乎是新的。

A : Yes, I know it is. But ...

　　是的，我知道它是。但是…

B : And you promised that you'd buy it. I really need to sell it.

　　你答應過要買的。我真的得賣。

A : My point is the price is too high.

　　我的意思是價錢太高了。

B : Oh! Well, maybe I could lower the price.

　　哦！好吧，或許我可以降低價錢。

〔舉一反三〕

A : Let's get to the point. What do you want?

　　我們談重點。你要什麼？

B : I want a vacation.

　　我要休假。

A : It's a beautiful house. You should buy it.

　　這是間漂亮的房子。你該買的。

B : Yes, but my point is that I can't afford it.

　　是，但重要的是我買不起。

A : So, since I have more experience, I should be paid more.

　　既然我的經驗較多，我應該得到更多的報酬。

B : All right, I see your point.

　　好的，我知道你的意思了。

A : You've been talking all night, but I don't see your point.

　　你整晚一直在說，但是我不明白你的要點。

B : My point is that you should get a job.

　　我的要點是，你該找份工作。

A : He talks a lot, but I never understand him.

　　他說得很多，但是我從不了解他。

B : That's because there's no point to what he says.

　　那是因為他說的沒有要點。

【註釋】

employee〔ɪmˈplɔɪ·i, ˌɛmplɔɪˈi〕*n.* 職員；雇員

get to the point 說到要點

15. *Keep that in mind.*

Dialogue 1

A : Have you gone for that job interview at the department store?

你去了那家百貨公司的面試嗎？

B : Not yet. My appointment is tomorrow.

還沒。我約定的時間是明天。

A : You have the experience. You should do all right.

你有經驗。你應該沒問題的。

B : I hope so, anyway. 無論如何，我希望如此。

A : Remember, they want someone who works well with people.

記住，他們要一個能和大家合作的人。

B : Yes, I'll keep that in mind.

是的，我會記住的。

Dialogue 2

A : Jack, we have a dinner date with the Johnsons tonight.

傑克，今晚我們和強生家有個晚餐的約會。

B : I'm glad you reminded me. When and where?

我很高興你提醒我。幾點在哪裡？

A : We're meeting them at 7:30 P.M. at the "Asiaworld Plaza".

我們七點半和他們在環亞大飯店見面。

B : We have to try to sell Mr. Johnson on our product. Please keep that in mind when speaking with Mrs. Johnson.

我們得試著把產品賣給強生先生。和強生太太談話的時候，請記得這點。

A : I'll try my best.
　　我會盡力而爲的。

B : I know you will.
　　我知道你會的。

Dialogue 3

A : I've sent out the invitations for our dinner party.
　　我已經發出了晚宴的邀請。

B : Now we have to plan the menu.
　　現在我們得計畫一下菜單。

A : Keep in mind that Mrs. Smith is a vegetarian.
　　記住史密斯太太吃素。

B : Right. I have a salad in mind for her.
　　是的。我爲她想好了一道沙拉。

A : And I hope you remembered to invite your sister.
　　我希望你記得邀請你姊姊。

B : Oh, I forgot! It slipped my mind.
　　哦，我忘了！忘得一乾二淨。

〔舉一反三〕

A : You have an appointment with your doctor tomorrow.
　　你明天和你的醫生有個約定。

B : Yes, I'll keep that in mind.
　　是的，我會記住的。

A : Please keep in mind that you should speak slowly
　　and clearly.
　　請記得你該說得慢而且清楚。

B : I'll try my best.
　　我會盡力而爲的。

A : Don't forget to bring your camera this weekend.
　　這週末別忘了帶你的相機來。
B : Sure. I'll keep it in mind.
　　當然，我會記住的。

A : Do you have anything in mind for Jane's birthday
　　present?
　　你想好要送珍什麼生日禮物嗎？
B : Yes, I think I'll get her a sweater.
　　是的，我想我要給她一件毛線衣。

A : Did you remember that the Johnsons invited us to
　　dinner?
　　你記得強生家邀我們吃晚飯嗎？
B : No, it slipped my mind.
　　不，我忘了。

【註釋】

keep ~ in mind 記住~
Asiaworld Plaza 環亞大飯店
menu (ˈmɛnju, ˈmenju) *n.* 菜單
vegetarian (ˌvɛdʒəˈtɛrɪən) *n.* 素食者
sweater (ˈswɛtə) *n.* 毛線衣

16. That was a close call.

Dialogue 1

A : Thank you very much! That guy is crazy.
非常感謝你！那個人瘋了。

B : I agree. That was a close all. Another inch and you'd be dead.
我同意。那真是千鈞一髮。再近一吋，你就死了。

A : He didn't even look back.
他甚至沒回頭看。

B : Some people just don't care how they drive.
有些人就是不在乎他們怎麼開車。

A : Well, thanks again for grabbing me.
再次謝謝你抓住我。

B : Don't mention it. I'm glad you're all right.
不客氣。我很高興你沒事。

Dialogue 2

A : I'm lucky I got here in time.
我很幸運及時到這裡。

B : Why is that? 為什麼？

A : I almost missed my train.
我差點錯過火車了。

B : What happened? 怎麼回事？

A : Well, my alarm clock didn't go off. I had to skip breakfast and run to the train station.
我的鬧鐘沒響。我得省掉早餐，跑到火車站。

B : That was a close call.
那真是千鈞一髮。

Dialogue 3

A : Boy, do I have a tight schedule today?
好傢伙，我今天的時間表很緊湊嗎？

B : Right. You're going to be very busy.
是的。你會非常忙。

A : First I have to take my wife to work at 8:30.
首先，我八點半得帶我太太去上班。

B : Then, you'll have to rush downtown to pick up your passport.
然後，你得趕到市中心去拿你的護照。

A : And then, I have to make my 9:45 flight at the airport.
然後，我得去機場搭九點四十五分的飛機。

B : Wow! That's cutting it close.
哇！那真緊湊。

〔舉一反三〕

A : That guy almost hit my car.
那個人幾乎撞到我的車子。

B : I'll say. That was a close call.
一點也不錯。那真是千鈞一髮。

A : I almost caught the flu from my wife.
我差一點給我太太傳染流行感冒了。

B : You had a close call.
你真險。

A : That bus nearly didn't stop for us.
那公車差點沒停。

B : Right. That was close.
是的。差點。

A : Bob has a tight schedule this week.
　　鮑伯這週的時間表很緊湊。

B : He's going to be cutting it close.
　　他將很緊迫。

A : I have to work until 6 tonight and be at the
　　show at 6:25.
　　我今晚得工作到六點，六點二十五分去看表演。

B : That's cutting it close.
　　那很緊迫。

【註釋】

close call 千鈞一髮
skip〔skɪp〕*vt.* 省略
boy〔bɔɪ〕*interj.* 好傢伙！真是！（表驚訝）
pick up 得到
passport〔'pæs,port , -,pɔrt〕*n.* 護照
I'll say. 是的；一點也不錯。
flu〔flu〕*n.* 流行性感冒

17. *Bumper to bumper.*

Dialogue 1

A : What took you so long?
什麼事使你耽擱了這麼久?

B : Traffic on the freeway is bumper to bumper.
高速公路上的交通大排長龍。

A : That's unusual for this time of the day.
那在白天的這個時候是少有的。

B : I know. There was an accident earlier in the day. I think that's why.
我知道。早上有件車禍。我想那就是原因。

A : That could be.
可能是。

B : Well, we'd better stop talking and get going. We're late already.
嗯,我們最好停止說話,出發吧。我們已經遲了。

Dialogue 2

A : When is the best time to drive home?
什麼時候開車回家最好?

B : Well, it's good to avoid rush hour if you can.
嗯,如果你能的話,最好避免尖峰時間。

A : When's that?
尖峰時間是什麼時候?

B : Rush hour is usually between four and six in the afternoon.
尖峰時間通常是下午四點到六點間。

A : That's when everyone gets off work.
　　那是大家下班的時候。

B : Right. Traffic is always bumper to bumper then.
　　是的。那時候交通總是大排長龍。

Dialogue 3

A : I was lucky going home yesterday.
　　昨天回家時我很幸運。

B : Why, what happened? 怎麼回事？

A : It only took me twenty minutes to drive home.
　　我只花了二十分鐘就開到家了。

B : Twenty minutes on a Friday afternoon? Usually it takes twice as long.
　　禮拜五下午只花二十分鐘？通常要花兩倍時間的。

A : But I took a different route, and the traffic was very light.
　　但是我走不同的路，而交通量很小。

B : You are lucky. Traffic was at a standstill on the expressway.
　　你很幸運。昨天高速公路上交通阻塞。

〔舉一反三〕

A : Why are you so late?
　　你為什麼這麼晚？

B : I'm sorry. The traffic was bumper to bumper.
　　對不起。交通大排長龍。

A : I hate this rush hour traffic.
　　我討厭尖峰時間的交通。

B : Yes, it takes so long to get home.
　　是的，要花那麼久的時間才到家。

A : I heard there was a bad accident on expressway.
　我聽說高速公路上有件嚴重的車禍。

B : Right. Traffic was at a standstill.
　是的。交通阻塞了。

A : Did it take you long to drive downtown?
　你花了很久的時間才開到市中心嗎?

B : No, traffic was unusually light.
　沒有，交通量反常地少。

A : I heard that northbound traffic is at a crawl.
　我聽說往北的交通前進緩慢。

B : Maybe I'll take a different route home.
　或許我會走另一條路回去。

【註釋】

freeway (ˈfriˌwe) *n.* 高速公路 (行駛速度大約 100 哩)

bumper (ˈbʌmpɚ) *n.* (車輛前後的) 緩衝檔

bumper to bumper 汽車一輛緊接一輛排長龍；保險桿幾乎碰保險桿

rush hour 尖峰時間

standstill (ˈstændˌstɪl) *n.* 停頓

expressway (ɪkˈsprɛsˌwe , ɛk-) *n.* 高速公路 (行駛速度大約 45 哩)

northbound (ˈnɔrθˌbaʊnd) *adj.* 往北的

crawl (krɔl) *n.* 緩慢前進

18. *Chances are slim*.

Dialogue 1

A : What are your chances of getting into Harvard?
你進哈佛的機會如何?

B : My chances are slim.
我的機會很小。

A : I hear those Ivy League College are tough to get into.
我聽說那些常春藤盟校很難進。

B : I know. I'd have a better chance at the state university.
我知道。我進州立大學的機會會大一點。

A : Sure. It's not a bad school, either.
當然。那個學校也不壞。

B : I'd rather be a big fish in a small pond.
我寧可做小池塘裡面的大魚。

Dialogue 2

A : Do you think the Bears will go to the Superbowl?
你認為熊隊會得冠軍嗎?

B : No, chances are slim.
不會,機會很小。

A : You're right. They're a weak team, defensively.
對。他們隊的防禦很弱。

B : What are New York's chances?
紐約隊的機會呢?

A : A little better. They have some good rookies this year.

好一點。他們今年有些好的新手。

B : We'll wait and see.

我們等著瞧。

Dialogue 3

A : What do you think of the mayoral election?

你對市長選舉有什麼看法？

B : I think Wilson has a good chance.

我認爲威爾森機會很大。

A : What about Bradley?

布萊德雷呢？。

B : He doesn't have a chance.

他沒機會。

A : I disagree. He's had more experience.

我不同意。他經驗比較豐富。

B : But he's too old. The voters want a younger man like Wilson.

但是他太老了。投票的人要一個像威爾森一樣，比較年輕的人。

〔舉一反三〕

A : Is Bob going to get a raise?

鮑伯要加薪了嗎？

B : No, his chances are slim.

不，他的希望很小。

A : What are your chances of getting that job?

你得到那工作的機會如何？

B : I think I have a good chance.

我想我很有希望。

A : Do you think you'll get into the University?

　　你認爲你進得了那所大學嗎?

B : I'm not sure. My chances would be better if I had better grades.

　　我不確定。如果我的成績好一點，機會就比較大。

A : What are your chances of getting a vacation?

　　你休假的希望大嗎?

B : I don't have a chance; there's too much work.

　　我沒希望;有太多工作要做了。

A : What are Jone's chances in the election?

　　瓊在這次選舉中的機會如何?

B : His chances are about 50-50.

　　他的機會大約是五十對五十。

【註釋】

Harvard〔'hɑrvəd〕*n.* 哈佛大學

slim〔slɪm〕*adj.* 微少的

ivy〔'aɪvɪ〕*n.* 常春藤　Ivy League 常春藤盟校，即美國東北部八所著名的大學所組成的傳統聯盟，包括 Harvard, Yale, Princeton, Columbia, Dartmouth, Cornell, Pennsylvania 及 Brown 等。

tough〔tʌf〕*adj.* 困難的

Bears 美足球隊名稱

Superbowl 冠軍杯

defensively〔dɪ'fɛnsɪvlɪ〕*adv.* 防禦地;取守勢地

rookie〔'rʊkɪ〕*n.* 新手

mayoral〔'meərəl, 'mɛrəl〕*adj.* 市長的

Bradley〔'brædlɪ〕*n.* 布萊德雷

voter〔'votə〕*n.* 投票的人

19. Far from it.

Dialogue 1

A : Can you help me with my English homework? You're a genius.

你能幫我做我的英文家庭作業嗎？你是個天才。

B : Far from it, but I'll try to help you. What's your problem?

才不是呢，但我會試著幫忙你。你的問題是什麼？

A : I get mixed up with the past participle.

我被過去分詞搞糊塗了。

B : You simply have to memorize them.

你只要背下來就好了。

A : I know, but for some reason I just can't keep them straight in my mind.

我知道，但是因為某種原因，我就是沒辦法把它們清楚記牢。

B : O.K. Sit down and I'll go over them with you.

好的。坐下來，我和你一起複習一遍。

Dialogue 2

A : What'll we do tonight?

我們今晚要做什麼？

B : I know! I can cook dinner for you.

我知道！我能給你煮晚餐。

A : Are you a good cook?

你是個好廚師嗎？

B : No, far from it. But I do know how to make chili.

不，絕不是。但是我知道怎麼做辣味菜。

A : That's fine! I love chili.
那好！我很喜歡辣味菜。

B : The only problem is, I don't have any food in the house!
唯一的問題是，我家裡什麼食物也沒有！

Dialogue 3

A : Excuse me, John, can I ask you a question?
對不起，約翰，我能問你一個問題嗎？

B : Sure, if it's not personal.
當然，如果那不是私事的話。

A : No, it isn't personal. It's about politics.
不，那不是私事。是關於政治。

B : I'm afraid politics is beyond me.
我恐怕不懂政治。

A : Well, do you have any opinions on the president?
好吧，那麼你對主席有什麼意見？

B : No. I just wish him good luck.
沒有。我只希望他好運。

〔舉一反三〕

A : Can you type very fast?
你打字能打得很快嗎？

B : Far from it. I'm quite slow.
一點也不。我相當慢。

A : Isn't Mr. Dixson an expert in economics?
狄克森先生不是經濟學的專家嗎？

B : Far from it. He knows a little bit, but that's all.
一點也不。他知道一些，就那樣而已。

A : Can you help me bake bread?
　　你能幫我烤麵包嗎？

B : I'm far from being a baker, but I can help.
　　我絕不是個麵包師傅，但我能幫忙。

A : Do you know how to play the violin?
　　你會拉小提琴嗎？

B : No, that's beyond me.
　　不，我不會。

A : Can you mend my pants for me?
　　你能幫我補褲子嗎？

B : I'm sorry. I'm afraid sewing is beyond me.
　　抱歉。我不會縫紉。

《背景説明》

　　Far from it. 「絕對沒那回事。」可用來表示強烈的否認或謙虛的推辭。因此，有人説：I hear you drink a lot. 可用 ***Far from it.*** I don't touch liquor. 回答。對於稱讚的話，如：I hear you're a good singer. 則可用 ***Far from it.*** I can't carry a tune. 回答。

　　如果表示一點能力也沒有，可用 ***beyond***。如：回答 Can you cook? 可用 No, I'm afraid cooking is ***beyond*** me. 來表示一點也不會。

【註釋】

far from 一點也不；遠非　　***mix up*** 使混亂
participle〔ˋpɑrtəsəp!, ˋpɑrtsəp!〕*n.* 分詞
go over 複習　　chili〔ˋtʃɪlɪ〕*n.* 乾辣椒
beyond *sb.* 超出某人；為某人能力所不及　　expert〔ˋɛkspɚt〕*n.* 專家
baker〔ˋbekɚ〕*n.* 麵包師傅　　sewing〔ˋsoɪŋ〕*n.* 縫紉

20. *I'm behind in my work.*

Dialogue 1

A : Why did you come home so late last night?
　　你昨晚為什麼那麼晚回家？

B : I had to stay at the office.
　　我得留在辦公室。

A : Why?
　　為什麼？

B : I'm so behind in my work, it'll take several evenings to catch up.
　　我工作進度落後很多，要花幾個晚上才趕得上。

A : Is there anything I can help you with?
　　有什麼我能幫你做的嗎？

B : I wish there was.
　　我但願有。

Dialogue 2

A : How are you doing this semester?
　　你這學期功課怎樣？

B : Not as good as last year. I'm behind in my studies.
　　不像去年那麼好。我讀書進度落後了。

A : Really? You're usually very conscientious.
　　真的？你通常都很盡責的。

B : But I was in the hospital for almost two weeks.
　　但是我在醫院待了將近兩週。

[圖] *20. I'm behind in my work.* 59

A : Oh, I'm sorry to hear that.

　　哦，聽到那件事我很難過。

B : I couldn't get any studying done.

　　我沒辦法完成任何功課。

Dialogue 3

A : I hear Joe had to go small claims court.

　　我聽說喬得上小額欠款法庭。

B : What for?

　　為什麼？

A : He bought a car, but he got behind in his payments.

　　他買了一輛車子，但是他拖欠付款。

B : That's pretty bad. Usually he pays his bills.

　　那很糟。通常他付帳的。

A : Yes, but he lost his job.

　　是的，但是他失業了。

B : That's a shame.

　　那真可憐。

〔 舉一反三 〕

A : Why are you working this weekend?

　　你這週末為什麼工作呢？

B : I'm behind in my work.

　　我工作進度落後了。

A : Did you finish writing your book?

　　你寫完你的書了嗎？

B : No, I've gotten behind.

　　不，我進度落後了。

A : Have you completed your classwork yet?
　　你在教室做的功課做完了嗎？

B : No, I'm a little behind in my studies.
　　沒有，我的功課落後了一點。

A : Are you ready to play the piano for us?
　　你準備好要爲我們彈琴嗎？

B : No, not yet. I'm behind in my practicing.
　　不，還沒有。我練習的進度落後了。

A : I hear Frank is behind in his rent.
　　我聽說富蘭克拖欠房租。

B : That's a shame.
　　那眞可恥。

【註釋】

　　behind〔bɪˈhaɪnd〕*adv.* 落後；拖欠
　　catch up 趕上
　　conscientious〔ˌkɑnʃɪˈɛnʃəs〕*adj.* （指行動或工作）謹愼的；盡責的
　　small claims court 小額欠款法庭，如果有人欠你房租，就可以上這種法庭告他。
　　classwork〔ˈklæsˌwɝk, ˈklɑs-〕*n.* 在教室做的功課

21. Not on your life!

Dialogue 1

A : You had your car fixed last week, didn't you?
你上週去修車了，不是嗎？

B : Yes, but I'm still having trouble starting it.
是的，但是我發動還是有困難。

A : Why don't you buy my car? I'm buying a new one and I have to get rid of it.
你何不買我的車子呢？我要買輛新車，舊的要脫手。

B : How much are you asking?
你開價多少？

A : $ 500.00.
五百元。

B : You want me to pay you $500.00 for that pile of junk? Not on your life!
你要我花五百元買一堆破爛嗎？絕不！

Dialogue 2

A : I'm very excited about graduation!
我對畢業很興奮！

B : I should think so.
我想是吧。

A : And I'm going to the graduation dance with Jim.
我要和吉姆去畢業舞會。

B : Jim? I thought you were going with Bill.
吉姆？我以爲妳要和比爾去的。

A : Not on your life! Bill and I are through.

絕不！比爾和我已經完了。

B : Sometimes I think you're very fickle.

有時候我認爲妳很善變。

Dialogue 3

A : I heard you had an argument with your supervisor.

我聽說你和你的主管有爭執。

B : Yeah. He wants me to work more overtime.

是的。他要我多加班。

A : Well, don't you want the money?

噢，你不想要錢嗎？

B : The money's O.K., but I need my free time, too.

錢是要，但是我也需要自己的時間。

A : Why don't you work overtime for just one month?

你何不只加班一個月呢？

B : No way! Forty hours a week, and that's it!

絕不！一週四十個鐘頭，就這麼多了！

〔舉一反三〕

A : I can sell you my stereo for $300.

我能以三百元把我的音響設備賣給你。

B : Three hundred? Not on your life!

三百？絕不！

A : I think you should complain to your boss.

我想你該對你的老闆發牢騷。

B : Not on your life! He might fire me.

絕不！他可能會開除我。

A : Are you going to ask Janet for a date?

你要和珍妮特約會嗎?

B : No way! Janet and I are through.

絕不!珍妮特和我完了。

A : Do you think you can work overtime tonight?

你認為你今晚能加班嗎?

B : No way! I'm going out tonight.

絕不!我今晚要出去。

A : Do you want to see the movie at the Hoover?

你想看豪華的那部電影嗎?

B : Not on your life. That movie's terrible.

絕不。那部電影很糟。

【註釋】

get rid of 除去;脫手

junk 〔dʒʌŋk〕 *n.* 破爛物

not on your life 絕不

fickle 〔'fɪkl̩〕 *adj.* 不專的;多變的

supervisor 〔ˌsjupə'vaɪzə〕 *n.* 管理者

no way 絕不

stereo 〔'stɛrɪo, 'stɪrɪo〕 *n.* 立體音響設備

22. *It's a pain in the neck.*

Dialogue 1

A : Is Janice working overtime tonight?
   珍妮絲今晚加班嗎?

B : Yes, because the second shift person is late.
   是的,因爲第二班的人來晚了。

A : Does she get paid for it?
   她有加班費嗎?

B : No, she doesn't.
   不,她沒有。

A : That's a real pain in the neck.
   那眞是難過的事。

B : She doesn't want to do it, but she has to.
   她不想加班,但是必須加。

Dialogue 2

A : I had to get up earlier than usual this morning.
   我今天早上得比平常早起。

B : Why's that?
   爲什麼?

A : The buses have been running late this week.
   這週公車一直晚到。

B : They're always slow in the winter.
   他們冬天老是慢來。

A : If I don't get up early, then I'm late for work.
   如果我不早起,我上班就遲到了。

B : That's a pain in the neck.
   那眞是難過的事。

Dialogue 3

A : What are you doing?
　　你在做什麼？

B : I'm cleaning the halls in my apartment building.
　　我在清掃我公寓大樓的大廳。

A : Doesn't the janitor usually do that?
　　那通常不是工友做的嗎？

B : Yes, but he's gone on vacation.
　　是的，可是他去休假了。

A : And so there's nobody to do it.
　　所以就沒人做了。

B : Right. It's a pain in the neck.
　　是的。那是件痛苦的事。

〔舉一反三〕

A : My car didn't start. I had to walk home from the store.
　　我的汽車發動不了。我得從商店走回家。

B : That's a pain in the neck.
　　那真是難過的事。

A : Wasn't Jack absent from work again?
　　傑克又沒來上班？

B : Yes. It's a drag, because I have to do his work.
　　是的。那是累贅，因為我得做他的工作。

A : Isn't it a pain in the neck when the bus is late?
　　公車遲來的時候，不是很痛苦嗎？

B : Yes, it's very inconvenient.
　　是的，那很不方便。

A：Do the trains often run slow in Chicago?

　　芝加哥的火車通常開得很慢嗎？

B：Only when there's heavy snow.

　　只有在下大雪的時候。

A：It's a real drag when I have to work Sundays.

　　星期天還要工作，真是累人。

B：Right. You need a day to relax.

　　是的。你需要一天來輕鬆一下。

【註釋】

　　shift〔ʃɪft〕n. 輪值；換班

　　pain in the neck 非常棘手的事；非常難對付的人

　　janitor〔'dʒænətɚ〕n. 管理員；清潔工；工友

　　drag〔dræg〕n. 拖累

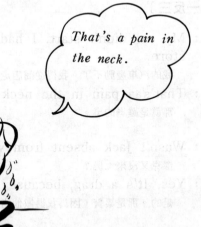

That's a pain in the neck.

23. Someone broke into my trunk.

Dialogue 1

A : Chicago Police.
芝加哥警察局。

B : I'd like to report a theft.
我想要報一件偷竊案。

A : What happened?
發生了什麼事?

B : Someone broke into my trunk.
有人開了我的行李箱。

A : What's missing? 掉了什麼?

B : I don't know. I can't get it open.
我不知道。我打不開它。

Dialogue 2

A : What happened to your car?
你的車怎麼了?

B : Someone broke into my trunk last night.
昨晚有人開了我的行李箱。

A : Did they get anything?
他們拿了什麼東西?

B : They took my spare tire.
他們拿了我的備胎。

A : Did you report it to the police and your insurance company?
你報告警察和你的保險公司了嗎?

B : Yes, I did. 是的,我報告了。

Dialogue 3

A : Did you notice my store window?
　你有沒有注意到我的櫥窗？

B : No. Why?
　沒有。怎麼了？

A : Someone broke it.
　有人打破它了。

B : When?
　什麼時候？

A : During the night, I guess.
　我想是在夜裡。

B : You'd better call the police right away.
　你最好馬上打電話給警察。

〔舉一反三〕

A : Someone broke into my car while it was parked in the garage.
　我的車子停在汽車間的時候，被人打開了。

B : Did you lose anything?
　你有沒有任何損失？

A : Someone broke into my house while I was on vacation.
　我休假的時候，有人闖入我的房子。

B : Did you have your lights on a timer?
　你的電燈有沒有上定時開關？

A : Jimmy, where did you get all that money?
　吉米，你從哪裡弄來那些錢？

B : I broke open my piggy bank.
　我把我的豬型撲滿打開了。

A : What happened to your car door?

你的車門怎麼了？

B : Someone punched out the door lock.

有人把門上的鎖撬開了。

A : I'd like to report a burglary.

我要報一件夜盜案。

B : Where are you calling from?

你從哪裡打來的？

***

【註釋】

break into 闖入，在此當「打開」。

trunk〔trʌŋk〕*n.* (汽車的) 行李箱 (車後放行李、用具的地方)

spare tire 備胎

garage〔gəˈraʒ, gəˈradʒ〕*n.* 汽車間；車庫

timer〔ˈtaɪmɚ〕*n.* 定時開關

piggy bank 豬型撲滿

punch〔pʌntʃ〕*vi.* 敲打

burglary〔ˈbɝglərɪ〕*n.* 夜盜；夜賊

24. I'm returning Mr. Brown's call.

Dialogue 1

A : Hello, China Airlines.
　　哈囉，中華航空公司。

B : This is Mr. Bok from Taiwan University.
　　我是台大的柏克先生。

A : Can I help you?
　　我能為你服務嗎？

B : I'm returning Mr. Brown's call.
　　我是回布朗先生的電話。

A : All right. I'll connect you with Mr. Brown.
　　好的。我給你接布朗先生。

B : Thank you. 謝謝你。

Dialogue 2

A : Good afternoon, Susan Tillman speaking.
　　午安，我是蘇珊‧提爾曼。

B : Hello, this is June Wallace. I'm returning your call.
　　哈囉，我是茱恩‧華萊士。我回妳的電話。

A : Hello, Miss Wallace. I'm glad I got a hold of you.
　　哈囉，華萊士小姐。我很高興和妳聯絡上。

B : What can I do for you?
　　我能為妳做什麼？

A : Are you still looking for a part-time secretary?
　　妳還在找兼差的秘書工作嗎？

B : Yes, I am.
　　是的，我在找。

Dialogue 3

A : Hello. Can I speak to the supervisor?
哈囉。請找主管聽電話好嗎？

B : Mr. Eliot is in conference. Can I take a message?
艾略特先生正在開會。要我留話嗎？

A : No, I have to speak to him myself.
不用，我得親自和他說。

B : Shall I have him return your call?
要不要請他回你的電話？

A : Please do.
好的。

B : What is your name and telephone number?
請問你叫什麼名字？你的電話號碼幾號？

〔舉一反三〕

A : Hello, Mr. Smith's office.
哈囉，這是史密斯先生辦公室。

B : I'm returning Mr. Smith's call.
我是回史密斯先生的電話。

A : Do you have some time to talk?
你有時間談話嗎？

B : No, I don't. Can I return your call later?
不，我沒有。我待會兒再回你的電話好嗎？

A : I'm sorry, Ms. Simpson isn't in her office now.
抱歉，辛普森女士現在不在她的辦公室。

B : That's all right. I'll get back to her later.
沒關係。我待會兒再打來。

A : Can I speak to the manager?
　　請找經理聽電話好嗎？

B : Hang on. I'll connect you with Mr. Wayne.
　　不要掛。我給你接威恩先生。

A : Jane is busy. Can I take a message?
　　珍很忙。要我留話嗎？

B : Yes, please have her return my call.
　　是的，請她回電話給我。

【註釋】

Wallace (ˈwɒlɪs) n. 華萊士
part-time (ˈpɑrtˈtaɪm) adj. 兼差的
conference (ˈkɑnfərəns) n. 會議
Eliot (ˈɛlɪət, ˈɛliət) n. 艾略特
Ms. (mɪz) n. 女士（代替 Miss 或 Mrs.，尤其當婚姻狀態不詳或無關緊要時）
Wayne (wen) n. 威恩

I'm returning Mr. Brown's call.

25. *We are in the same boat.*

Dialogue 1

A : Are you taking a vacation this summer?
   你今年夏天要休假嗎？

B : Yes, but we're not going anywhere.
   是的，但是我們哪兒也不去。

A : What do you mean?
   你的意思是什麼？

B : Everything is sky high. We don't have enough money for a vacation. How about you?
   一切都很貴。我們沒有足夠的錢去度假。你們呢？

A : We're in the same boat. With both boys in college, it's been tough. We simply can't afford a vacation this year.
   我們處境相同。因為兩個男孩都在唸大學，經濟一直很困難。我們今年就是沒辦法去度假。

B : Maybe next year things will be better.
   或許明年情況會好轉。

Dialogue 2

A : How was your day?
   你的日子過得怎樣？

B : Terrible! I'm so bored with my job, I could scream!
   可怕！我對工作煩透了，我真想尖叫！

A : I know just how you feel. I'm tired of doing the same thing day after day.
   我知道你的感覺。我厭倦每天做一樣的事。

B : Have you spoken to your boss about it?
   你和你的老板談了這件事嗎？

A : I'm afraid to. He might tell me to look for another job.

我怕去談。他可能會要我另外找工作。

B : I'm in the same boat. 我和你的處境相同。

Dialogue 3

A : I hear you're studying English at night.

我聽說你晚上在學英文。

B : That's right. I haven't been able to get a good job because my pronunciation is poor.

是的。因為我的發音不好，一直找不到好工作。

A : I'm in the same boat. What should I do?

我的處境相同。我該怎麼辦？

B : Why don't you come to class with me?

你何不和我一起上課？

A : That's a good idea. When can I start?

那是個好主意。我什麼時候可以開始？

B : How about tonight? I'll pick you up at six.

今晚如何？我六點來接你。

〔舉一反三〕

A : My boss didn't give me a raise.

我的老板不給我加薪。

B : I'm in the same boat. Neither did mine.

我的處境相同。我的老板也不給我加。

A : I can't stand this food!

我無法忍受這食物！

B : I feel the same way. I'd rather eat Chinese food any day!

我有同感。我寧可天天吃中國菜。

A : I have a terrible headache! My children were listening to rock music all evening.

我頭痛得很厲害！我的小孩整晚聽搖滾樂。

B : I know just how you feel.

我知道你的感覺。

A : I was going to buy a car, but I haven't been able to save enough money.

我本來要買輛車子，但是我沒辦法存足夠的錢。

B : I know what you mean.

我知道你的意思。

A : I'd like to go to an American restaurant, but I don't know what to order.

我想去家美式餐廳，但是我不知道要點什麼。

B : I'm in the same boat.

我的處境相同。

【註釋】

sky high 極昂貴的

in the same boat 處境相同

tough〔tʌf〕*adj.* 困難的

be bored with 對～厭煩

scream〔skrim〕*vi.* 尖叫

day after day 日復一日

pick up 搭載

26. My mouth is watering.

Dialogue 1

A : Do you like Italian food?
你喜歡義大利食物嗎？

B : Oh yes, I love it.
是的，我很喜歡。

A : Well, I know a very good place in this neighborhood.
我知道附近有個好地方。

B : Do they have good spaghetti?
他們的義大利麵好嗎？

A : It's excellent. 棒極了。

B : My mouth is watering. Let's go!
我在流口水了。我們走吧！

Dialogue 2

A : Would you like to eat at my parent's tonight?
你今晚想到我父母家吃飯嗎？

B : Is your mother a good cook?
你媽媽是個好廚師嗎？

A : She sure is..
她當然是。

B : Doesn't she make a good potato salad?
她馬鈴薯沙拉是不是做得很好？

A : Right. It'll make your mouth water.
是的。那會讓你流口水。

B : I feel hungry already.
我已經覺得餓了。

Dialogue 3

A : I think we should get something to eat.
我想我們該找些吃的。

B : Are you hungry?
你餓了嗎？

A : Hungry? I'm starving.
餓？我餓死了。

B : There's a Hu Nan restaurant near here.
附近有家湖南菜館。

A : Is the food very hot?
菜很辣嗎？

B : It's kind of hot, but it's very tasty.
有一點辣，但是味道很好。

〔舉一反三〕

A : We have some chocolate cake for dessert.
我們有巧克力蛋糕做甜點。

B : Great! My mouth is watering.
真棒！我在流口水了。

A : This pizza will make your mouth water.
這義大利脆餅會讓你流口水。

B : I can't wait to have some.
我等不及想吃了。

A : Do you like this restaurant?
你喜歡這家餐廳嗎？

B : Yes, the food is very tasty.
是的，菜很好吃。

A : Are you hungry?
　　你餓了嗎？

B : Hungry? I'm famished.
　　餓？我餓壞了。

A : Is this food too hot?
　　這菜太辣了嗎？

B : Yes, it's too hot for me.
　　是的，對我來說太辣了。

【註釋】

spaghetti〔spəˈgɛtɪ〕n. 義大利麵

water〔ˈwɔtɚ , ˈwɑtɚ〕vi. 流口水

starve〔stɑrv〕vi. 餓死

kind of 有一點；有幾分

pizza〔ˈpitsə〕n. 義大利脆餅；披薩

famish〔ˈfæmɪʃ〕vi. 挨餓

27. Can you give me a rain check on that?

Dialogue 1

A : Hi, Chuck. I'd like to take you out to dinner sometime next week.

嗨，契克。我下週想找個時間帶你去吃晚飯。

B : I don't think I can make it next week. Can you give me a rain check on that?

我想我下週沒辦法。你以後再帶我去好嗎？

A : Would the following week be all right with you?

再下一週可以嗎？

B : Fine. That would work out real well.

好的。那會很好。

A : Any particular place you'd like to go?

你有沒有想去什麼特別的地方？

B : Come to think of it, there is a good Chinese restaurant nearby.

讓我想想，附近有家好的中國餐館。

Dialogue 2

A : My brother and his family will be coming into town next week.

我弟弟和他的家人下週要到城裡來。

B : Is he the one who writes articles for the China Times?

他是替中國時報寫文章的那一位嗎？

A : Right. Why don't you come over next Sunday to meet him?

　　是的。你何不下星期天來見見他呢？

B : I'd love to, but I can't. Can you give me a rain check?

　　我很想來，但是沒辦法來。你改天再請我好嗎？

A : Sure. They'll be here for a week, so just let me know when you can come.

　　當然。他們會在這裡留一星期，所以告訴我，你什麼時候能來。

B : O.K. I'll be very interested in seeing him.

　　好的。我很有興趣見見他。

Dialogue 3

A : Will you and Bob be able to come to the meeting Tuesday?

　　你和鮑伯星期二能來開會嗎？

B : No, I'm afraid not. Something's come up.

　　不能，我恐怕不能來。發生了一些事。

A : I'm sorry to hear that. I would be interested in having both of you there.

　　聽到那麼說，我很難過。我希望你們兩個都能來。

B : Perhaps you can give us a rain check.

　　或許你可以改天再請我們。

A : I'd like to, but we can only have the one meeting.

　　我很想這麼做，但是我們只能開一次會。

B : Maybe I can change my plans.

　　或許我可以改變我的計劃。

〔舉一反三〕

A : Can you give me a rain check on that?
　　你可以改天再請我嗎？

B : Sure. How about next Friday?
　　當然。下星期五如何？

A : I'm sorry. I can't go to the movies with you Saturday.
　　抱歉。我星期六沒辦法和你一起去看電影。

B : That's O.K. I'll give you a rain check.
　　沒關係。我改天再請你。

A : Will you be able to attend the meeting?
　　你能去開會嗎？

B : No, I won't. Something's come up.
　　不，我不能去。發生了一些事。

A : Would you be interested in seeing the new play?
　　你有興趣看那齣新話劇嗎？

B : Yes, I'd like to very much.
　　是的，我很想看。

A : It's very important for you to come.
　　你來很重要。

B : Maybe I can change my plans.
　　或許我能改變我的計劃。

【註釋】

　　rain check 被邀赴宴會因故不能到，而希望以後改期再請的要求。或是戶外比賽因雨而停止舉行時，散發給觀眾留待以後用的票。

28. *What do you recommend?*

Dialogue 1

A : Are you ready to order now?
你準備好要點什麼了嗎?

B : What do you recommend?
你推薦什麼?

A : Sirloin steak is our special of the day, sir.
腰肉上部的牛排是今天的特餐,先生。

B : All right. I'll have that.
好的。我就吃那個。

A : How do you want your steak?
你的牛排要怎樣的?

B : Medium, please.
請來七、八分熟的。

Dialogue 2

A : Excuse me, waiter.
對不起,服務生。

B : Yes, sir. Can I help you?
是的,先生。我能爲你服務嗎?

A : Do you have any fresh seafood today?
你們今天有任何新鮮海鮮嗎?

B : Yes, we have lake perch, trout, and lobster.
有。我們有湖裡的鱸魚、鱒魚和龍蝦。

A : I don't know. What do you recommend?
我不知道。你推薦什麼?

B : I'd recommend the perch, sir. It has a special sauce.
我推薦鱸魚,先生。它有特別的調味汁。

Dialogue 3

A : What's the special of the day?
今天的特餐是什麼？

B : Today, we have barbecued chicken.
今天我們有烤雞。

A : That sounds good. I can't decide between that and the roast beef.
似乎不錯。我沒辦法決定要烤雞，還是要烤牛肉。

B : I'd suggest the chicken, sir.
我建議烤雞，先生。

A : Well, I think I'd prefer the roast beef.
好吧，我想我還是比較喜歡烤牛肉。

B : All right. I'll be back with your coffee.
好的。我去給你拿咖啡。

〔舉一反三〕

A : What do you recommend?
你建議什麼？

B : Well, our omelettes are very popular.
我們的煎蛋捲很受歡迎。

A : What do you suggest for dessert?
你建議吃什麼甜點？

B : We have homemade apple pies.
我們有自製的蘋果派。

A : What's the specialty here?
這裡有什麼招牌菜？

B : We have excellent hamburgers.
我們有最好的漢堡。

A : How would you like your beef, sir?

　　先生，你的牛肉要怎樣的？

B : Medium, please.

　　請來六分到八分熟的。

A : Is everything all right, sir?

　　先生，一切都好嗎？

B : No, I'm afraid my meat is too tough.

　　不，我恐怕肉太老了。

――――――――――――――――――――――――――――――――

《背景説明》

　　　到餐館吃飯，如果對菜單内容不熟悉，想請服務生推薦好菜，可說：***What do you recommend?*** 或是***What's your specialty?*** ***What's the special of the day?*** 服務生則可回答：***I suggest ~.*** 或***I'd recommend ~.*** 如果接受了，就回答***I'll have that.***

【註釋】

order〔'ɔrdɚ〕*vi.* 點（食物）

recommend〔,rɛkə'mɛnd〕*vt.* 推薦；介紹

sirloin〔'sɝlɔɪn〕*n.* 牛腰上部的肉；沙朗牛排

seafood〔'si,fud〕*n.* 海產食物　　perch〔pɝtʃ〕*n.* 鱸魚

trout〔traʊt〕*n.* 鱒魚　　lobster〔'labstɚ〕*n.* 龍蝦

sauce〔sɔs〕*n.* 調味汁

barbecue〔'barbɪ,kju〕*vt.* 加佐料炙、烤　　roast〔rost〕*vt.* 烤

omelette〔'amlɪt〕*n.* 煎蛋捲（常以火腿、乳酪等作餡）（= *omelet*）

homemade〔'hom'med〕*adj.* 自製的

specialty〔'spɛʃəltɪ〕*n.* 招牌菜；特製品

29. I ache all over.

Dialogue 1

A : Hi, Bill. You're looking very good.
嗨，比爾。你看來很好。

B : Yeah, I joined a health club to keep in shape.
是的，我參加了一個健康俱樂部，以保持身材。

A : Do you exercise every day?
你每天做運動嗎？

B : Yes, I've been jogging for over 4 months now.
是的，我已經慢跑四個多月了。

A : I just started. I ache all over.
我才開始。我全身酸痛。

B : Yeah, I know. But it goes away.
是的，我知道。但是會過去的。

Dialogue 2

A : How do you like this disco?
你覺得這次狄斯可舞會如何？

B : I've never seen so many beautiful girls.
我從沒看過這麼多漂亮的女孩。

A : And the music is great.
而且音樂很棒。

B : But with all this dancing I ache all over.
但是我跳得全身酸痛。

A : Me too. Let's stop and order a drink.
我也是。我們停下來，叫點喝的。

B : All right. They're on me.
好的。我請客。

Dialogue 3

A : I haven't been feeling well recently.
　　我最近一直不太舒服。

B : What's the matter? Do you ache all over?
　　怎麼回事？你全身酸痛嗎？

A : No, it's a backache.
　　不，是背痛。

B : Where does it hurt?
　　哪裡痛？

A : It aches here, around my lower back.
　　這裡痛，我的下背。

B : Maybe you ought to see a doctor.
　　或許你該去看醫生。

〔舉一反三〕

A : Did you play tennis this afternoon?
　　你今天下午打網球了嗎？

B : Yes, and now I ache all over.
　　是的，而我現在全身酸痛。

A : Where exactly does it hurt?
　　究竟哪裡痛？

B : I can't say. I sort of ache all over.
　　我說不出來。我全身都有點酸痛。

A : What's the matter?
　　怎麼回事？

B : I have a terrible headache.
　　我頭痛得很厲害。

A : Where do you feel pain?
　　你哪裡覺得痛？

B : It hurts here, in my shoulder.
　　這裡痛，我的肩膀。

A : Do you exercise regularly?
　　你定期運動嗎？

B : Yes, every day. I want to keep in shape.
　　是的，每天。我想保持身材。

【註釋】

jog〔dʒɑg〕*vi.* 慢跑
disco〔'dɪsko〕*n.* 狄斯可
be on *sb.* 某人請客
backache〔'bæk͵ek〕*n.* 背痛
hurt〔hɜt〕*vi.* 疼痛
sort of 有幾分；有點

I just started.
I ache all over.

Yeah, I know.
But it goes
away.

30. I have a runny nose.

Dialogue 1

A : May I help you?
　　我能為你服務嗎？

B : Do you have something for a cold?
　　你有沒有感冒藥？

A : Do you have a fever?
　　你發燒嗎？

B : No, I just have a runny nose.
　　沒有。我只是流鼻涕。

A : Why don't you try an antihistamine?
　　你何不試試抗組胺劑？

B : That sounds like a good idea.
　　似乎是個好主意。

Dialogue 2

A : Your son wasn't in school today.
　　你的兒子今天沒上學。

B : No, Mrs. Golz. He had a runny nose.
　　沒有，高爾茲太太。他流鼻涕。

A : Does he have a temperature?
　　他發燒嗎？

B : No. I think he'll feel all right tomorrow.
　　沒有。我想他明天就會沒事的。

A : I'll give you his homework assignment.
　　我把他的家庭作業給你。

B : Thanks. I wouldn't want him to miss any schoolwork.
　　謝謝。我不希望他耽誤學校的功課。

Dialogue 3

A : What's wrong? You don't look well.
　　怎麼了？你看起來臉色不大好。

B : I feel terrible. I have a sore throat.
　　我覺得很不舒服。我喉嚨痛。

A : You should go home and get some sleep.
　　你該回家睡個覺。

B : I can't sleep, either. I have a splitting headache.
　　我也沒辦法睡。我頭痛得很厲害。

A : It sounds like you have something serious.
　　似乎你有什麼大病。

B : Really? Do you think I should see a doctor?
　　眞的？你認爲我該看醫生嗎？

〔 舉一反三 〕

A : What seems to be the problem?
　　大槪是什麼毛病呢？

B : I have a runny nose.
　　我流鼻涕。

A : I have a stuffed-up head and a sore throat.
　　我頭發脹，喉嚨痛。

B : Are you taking anything for it?
　　你有沒有吃藥？

A : Do you have a temperature?
　　你發燒嗎？

B : Yes, I have a slight fever.
　　是的，我有一點發燒。

A : You look sick.

　　你看起來生病了。

B : I think I'm catching a cold.

　　我想我感冒了。

A : I think I'd better see a doctor.

　　我想我最好去看醫生。

B : Why? Is it something serious?

　　為什麼？嚴重嗎？

【註釋】

runny (′rʌnɪ) *adj.* 流鼻涕的

antihistamine (,æntɪ′hɪstə,min) *n.* 抗組織胺

have a temperature 發燒

assignment (ə′saɪnmənt) *n.* 指定的工作

sore throat 喉嚨痛

splitting (′splɪtɪŋ) *adj.* 劇烈的

stuff (stʌf) *vt.* 填塞

31. It's out of the question.

Dialogue 1

A : I'm going to look at new cars tomorrow.
我明天要去看新車。

B : I wish I could afford one.
但願我買得起。

A : Why don't you come along?
你何不一起來?

B : I'd like to, but I don't want to be tempted.
我想去,但是我不想被引誘。

A : I'm sure you could get a good deal.
我想你能買到便宜貨。

B : No, buying a new car is out of the question for me right now.
不,我現在不可能買新車。

Dialogue 2

A : Did Jack invite you to his swimming party?
傑克邀你去他的游泳同樂會了嗎?

B : Swimming? It's too cold for swimming. He must be crazy.
游泳?天氣太冷了,不能游泳。他一定是瘋了。

A : So, you don't like to go swimming?
那麼,你不喜歡去游泳了?

B : Sure, I do. But swimming in this weather is out of the question.
我當然喜歡。但是這種天氣游泳是不可能的。

A : It's too bad you don't want to come. He's rented a heated indoor pool, you see.

你不想來太可惜了。你知道，他租了加熱的室內游泳池。

B : Oh, in that case, I'd love to come.

哦，在那種情況下，我很願意去。

Dialogue 3

A : Bob, we're going to have to lay you off.

鮑伯，我們得把你遣散了。

B : What? I can't afford to be laid off now.

什麼？我現在不能給遣散。

A : I'm sorry, Bob. But we can't afford to keep you.

對不起，鮑伯。但是我們供不起你。

B : But Mr. Schmidt, I've been a good employee, I just bought a new car....

但是士米德先生，我一直是個好雇員，我剛買了部新車…。

A : Bob, there's no question about it. We're laying you off next week.

鮑伯，這是一定的。我們下週就要遣散你了。

B : I'm going to talk to the union steward about this.

我要去找工會管理人談這件事。

〔 舉一反三 〕

A : Are you going to stay in your apartment?

你要住在你的公寓嗎？

B : Sure. Buying a house is out of the question for me.

當然。買一棟房子對我來說是不可能的。

A : So you didn't quit your job?
　　你沒辭職？

B : No! Finding a new job is out of the question these days.
　　沒有！最近找新工作是不可能的。

A : Should we invite Mary to the party?
　　我們要邀瑪莉來宴會嗎？

B : It's out of the question. I don't want to see her.
　　那是不可能的。我不想見她。

A : Is it important to learn English?
　　學英文重要嗎？

B : Of course! There's no question about it.
　　當然！那是一定的。

A : Isn't Jim going to get a scholarship?
　　吉姆不是要得到獎學金了嗎？

B : He definitely is. No question about it.
　　他當然是。沒問題的。

【註釋】

tempt〔tɛmpt〕*vt.* 引誘
deal〔dil〕*n.* 交易
out of the question 不可能 *cf.* ***out of question*** 無疑地
lay *sb.* ***off*** 暫時解雇某人；遣散
Schmidt〔ʃmɪt〕*n.* 士米德（姓）
employee〔ɪmˈplɔɪ.i , ͵ɛmplɔɪˈi〕*n.* 職員；雇員
union〔ˈjunjən〕*n.* 工會
steward〔ˈstjuwəd〕*n.* 管理人
scholarship〔ˈskɑlɚ͵ʃɪp〕*n.* 獎學金

32. Suit yourself.

Dialogue 1

A : I'd like to hear some music.
我想聽些音樂。

B : That sounds like fun.
那似乎有趣。

A : Would you rather listen to jazz or classical?
你想聽聽爵士樂還是古典的？

B : Suit yourself.
隨便。

A : I feel like classical.
我想聽古典的。

B : That's fine with me.
我同意。

Dialogue 2

A : There's a new movie showing at the Hoover theater.
豪華在演一部新片子。

B : Let's go tomorrow night.
我們明天晚上去看。

A : Can you pick me up?
你能來接我嗎？

B : Sure, what time?
當然，幾點？

A : Suit yourself.
隨便你。

B : I'll come over about 7 o'clock.
我大約七點過來。

Dialogue 3

A : Bob, can you help me this weekend?
　　鮑伯，你這個週末能幫忙我嗎？

B : What do you have to do?
　　你要做什麼？

A : I have to paint my apartment.
　　我得油漆我的公寓。

B : O.K. Should I come on Saturday or Sunday?
　　好的。要我星期六還是星期天去？

A : It doesn't matter to me. Suit yourself.
　　我無所謂。隨便你。

B : I think I'll come by on Sunday.
　　我想我星期天去。

〔舉一反三〕

A : Should I wear a tie to your party?
　　我去你的宴會要打領帶嗎？

B : Suit yourself.
　　隨你便。

A : Can I bring some friends to the picnic?
　　我可以帶些朋友去野餐嗎？

B : Sure. It's up to you.
　　當然。由你決定。

A : What time should I come over?
　　我該什麼時候過來？

B : It doesn't matter to me. Suit yourself.
　　我無所謂，隨你便。

A : Should I buy the brown shoes or the black shoes?
　　我該買咖啡色的鞋子或是黑色的鞋子？

B : It's up to you.
　　由你決定。

A : Do you want steak or chicken for dinner?
　　你晚餐想吃牛排還是雞肉？

B : I feel like steak tonight.
　　我今晚想吃牛排。

【註釋】

would rather 寧願

jazz〔dʒæz〕*n.* 爵士樂

Suit yourself. 隨你便。

feel like 想要

That's fine with me. 我同意；我可以；我沒問題。

pick up 搭載

come over 從遠處來

come by 造訪（= *call at* ）

Suit yourself.

I feel like steak tonight.

33. Once in a lifetime.

Dialogue 1

A : What do you think of the Pope's visit to the
United States?

你對教皇到美國訪問有什麼看法？

B : It's great. I'm anxious to see him.

太棒了。我渴望見他。

A : Are you going to attend the Papal mass?

你要去參加教皇主持的彌撒嗎？

B : Sure. It's a once in a lifetime opportunity.

當然。那是一生難得的機會。

A : Maybe I'll go, too.

也許我也會去。

B : You should. You'll never have a chance like this
again.

你該去的。你再也不會有這種機會。

Dialogue 2

A : Did you hear about Mary?

你有瑪莉的消息嗎？

B : No. What happened?

沒有。發生什麼事了？

A : Remember that she went to Hollywood a few
months ago?

記得她幾個月前去好萊塢嗎？

B : Yes, and she never came back.

記得，而她再也沒回來。

A : Well, she met a big television director, and now she's engaged to him!

　　嗯，她遇到一個電視大導演，現在和他訂婚了！

B : Wow! That happens only once in a lifetime!

　　哇！這種事一生只有一次！

Dialogue 3

A : Do you get out of the house very often?

　　你常出門嗎？

B : I used to, but I don't anymore.

　　我過去常出門，但現在不了。

A : Do you ever go to movies or plays?

　　你有沒有去看過電影或是話劇？

B : Once in a blue moon I'll see a movie.

　　我很少看電影。

A : Well, I think you should get out more.

　　那麼，我想你該多出去走走。

B : Maybe you're right.

　　或許你是對的。

〔舉一反三〕

A : Should I take that job in Europe?

　　我該接受歐洲的那份工作嗎？

B : Sure! It's a once in a lifetime opportunity.

　　當然！這是一生難得的機會。

A : I just won a new car in a contest!

　　我剛在一項比賽中贏了一輛新車！

B : Wow! That happens only once in a lifetime.

　　哇！那種事一生難得。

A ： I've got a free round-trip ticket to Hawaii!
我得到一張免費去夏威夷的來回機票！

B ： That's the chance of a lifetime.
那是一輩子難得的機會。

A ： Do you ever eat out?
你有沒有在外面吃過？

B ： Once in a blue moon.
很少。

A ： Do you want to see the movie at the Majesty?
你要看真善美的那部電影嗎？

B ： Not on your life. That movie's terrible.
絕不。那電影很糟。

【註釋】

Pope〔pop〕*n.* 羅馬敎皇
papal〔'pepḷ〕*adj.* 羅馬敎皇的
director〔dəˈrɛktɚ, daɪ-〕*n.* 電影、戲劇導演
once in blue moon 很少
wow〔waʊ〕*interj.* 哇！噢！（表示驚愕、愉快、痛苦等的感歎詞）
round-trip ticket 來回票

34. I can't pinpoint it.

Dialogue 1

A : My car isn't running very well.
我的車子跑得不怎麼好。

B : But you just bought it last month.
但是你上個月才買的。

A : I know, but sometimes it doesn't start.
我知道，但是有時候它發不動。

B : What's wrong with it?
它有什麼毛病？

A : I can't pinpoint it.
我沒辦法精確地指出來。

B : You'd better take it in to a mechanic.
你最好開進來給機工看看。

Dialogue 2

A : You speak English very well.
你的英文說得很好。

B : Thanks. I still have some difficulties, however.
謝謝。但是我仍然有些困難。

A : What kind of difficulties?
哪種困難？

B : Well, I have trouble understanding Americans.
嗯，我在了解美國人方面有困難。

A : Can you pinpoint the problem?
你能明確指出問題所在嗎？

B : I think it's because they speak so fast.
我想是因為他們說話太快了。

Dialogue 3

A : I've been losing money this year.
　　我今年錢一直在減少。

B : Really? What's the problem?
　　真的？有什麼問題？

A : I can't put my finger on it.
　　我找不出來。

B : Maybe you spend too much money for gas.
　　或許你花了太多油錢。

A : Or maybe I eat out too much.
　　也或許我太常到外面吃。

B : It's hard to say.
　　很難說。

〔舉一反三〕

A : What's wrong with your television set?
　　你的電視機有什麼毛病？

B : I can't pinpoint the problem
　　我沒辦法明確地指出來。

A : Does Tom know why he's been feeling sick?
　　湯姆知道他為什麼一直想吐嗎？

B : No, he can't pinpoint it.
　　不，他沒辦法弄清楚。

A : Why is your business losing money?
　　為什麼你的生意賠錢？

B : I can't put my finger on it.
　　我沒辦法找到原因。

A：Do you know why Ann quit her job?
　　你知道安為什麼辭職嗎？

B：No. It's hard to say.
　　不知道。這很難說。

A：Why is your car running so badly?
　　你的車子為什麼跑得這麼糟？

B：I can't say for sure.
　　我沒辦法肯定地說。

【註釋】

pinpoint〔'pɪn͵pɔɪnt〕*vi.* 精確指出
mechanic〔mə'kænɪk〕*n.* 機工
feel sick 噁心；想吐
put（*or lay*）*one's finger on* 明確指出
for sure 確定地

35. Give me some feedback.

Dialogue 1

A : Tom, I've been thinking about that Cadler job.
　　湯姆，我一直在想卡德樂的工作。

B : Oh? What will you do?
　　哦？你要怎麼辦？

A : Give me some feedback. I think I'd like to take it, if they would increase the pay.
　　給我一點建議。我想如果他們增加待遇，我願意接受這工作。

B : Gee, I don't know what you should do.
　　啊，我不知道你該怎麼辦。

A : Then, what would you do in my place?
　　那麼，如果你處在我的立場，你會怎麼做？

B : Well, I'd take the job anyway.
　　嗯，無論如何我會接受這工作。

Dialogue 2

A : I have a meeting this afternoon.
　　我今天下午有個會。

B : Oh, about what? 哦，是關於什麼的？

A : About my ideas for improving production.
　　關於我促進生產的構想。

B : Can you fill me in? I'm interested.
　　能告訴我嗎？我有興趣。

A : O.K. Maybe you can give me some feedback.
　　好的。或許你能給我點建議。

B : Yeah, before you tell the boss.
　　是啊，在你告訴老板之前。

Dialogue 3

A : What's up, Ed? You look down.
怎麼回事？愛德。你看來很沮喪。

B : Oh, my wife and I are really having problems.
噢，我太太和我真的有問題了。

A : Gee, that's too bad.
啊，那真不幸。

B : Can I talk to you for a minute? Maybe you can
give me some feedback.
我能和你談一會兒嗎？或許你能給我一點建議。

A : Sure, Ed.
當然，愛德。

B : Let's go for coffee.
我們去喝杯咖啡。

〔舉一反三〕

A : I just don't know what to do about that Thomas
case.
我就是不知道湯姆斯那件事要怎麼處理。

B : Tell me about it. Maybe I can give you some feedback.
告訴我，或許我能給你些意見。

A : I think we should go talk to Chris.
我想我們該去和克里斯談談。

B : Yeah, let's ask him for some feedback.
是啊，我們去問問他的意見。

A : I need some feedback on this situation.
這種情況我需要一些建議。

B : O.K., I'll ask what people think.
好的，我會問大家的看法。

A : I called you all in here because I need some feedback.

我把你們都聚集在這裏，因為我需要一些意見。

B : On what?

關於什麼的？

A : Have you made up your mind about the plan?

關於那計畫你決定好了嗎？

B : No, I can't seem to get any feedback on it.

沒有，我似乎得不到任何意見。

【註釋】

feedback〔'fid,bæk〕*n.* 回饋（本課中指告訴別人某事，而別人給你意見）

gee〔dʒi〕*interj.* 啊

yeah〔jɛ,jæ〕*adv.* = *yes*

Ed〔ɛd〕*n.* 男子名（ Edward, Edmund, Edwin 等之暱稱）

down〔daʊn〕*adj.* 沮喪的；意志消沉的

Chris〔krɪs〕*n.* 男子名為 Christopher 之暱稱；女子名為 Christine 的暱稱。

36. *Do you have any openings?*

Dialogue 1

A : May I help you?
我能為你服務嗎?

B : Yes. Do you have any openings for a typist?
是的。你有任何打字員的缺嗎?

A : How fast can you type?
你能打多快?

B : Sixty words per minute.
每分鐘六十字。

A : We have an opening in the sales department.
我們業務部門有個缺。

B : Thank you. May I come in for an interview?
謝謝你。我能進來面談一下嗎?

Dialogue 2

A : Bob's Auto Shop.
鮑伯汽車行。

B : Do you have any openings for a welder?
你們有銲工的缺嗎?

A : No. I'm sorry.
沒有,對不起。

B : Do you have any openings at all?
你們有任何空缺嗎?

A : No, we have nothing at the moment.
沒有,我們目前沒有。

B : Thank you, anyway.
無論如何,謝謝你。

Dialogue 3

A : Good morning. Western Fuel Supply.
早安。西部燃料供應公司。

B : Good morning. Personnel Department, please.
早安。請接人事部。

A : One moment, please, I'll connect you.
請等一下，我給你接。

B : Personnel Department. Miss James speaking.
人事部。我是詹姆斯小姐。

A : Good morning. Can you tell me if you have any secretarial openings?
早安。請告訴我，你們有秘書的缺嗎？

B : I'm sorry, we don't give out that information over the phone. You have to come in to our office and fill out an application.
抱歉，我們不在電話裡公布那種消息。你得來我們辦公室，並且填申請表。

〔舉一反三〕

A : Do you have any openings for part-time help?
你們有兼差傭人的缺嗎？

B : No, we don't.
不，我們沒有。

A : Are you looking for a position as a secretary?
你在找秘書的職位嗎？

B : I was, but I found one.
我本來在找，但是已經找到一個了。

A : We have a position in our Marketing Department. Are you interested?

我們行銷部門有個空缺。你有興趣嗎？

B : Yes, I'm interested.

是的，我有興趣。

A : Are you looking for any help?

你在找傭人嗎？

B : No. We don't need anyone right now.

不。我們現在不需要任何傭人。

A : I'd like to apply for the position of sales assistant.

我想申請業務助理的職位。

B : That position was just filled.

這職位剛被補上。

【註釋】

interview ('mtə,vju) n. 面談

welder ('wɛldə) n. 銲工

fuel ('fjuəl) n. 燃料

personnel (,pɜsn'ɛl) adj. 人事的

secretarial (,sɛkrə'tɛriəl) adj. 秘書的

give out 宣布；公布

fill out 填寫

application (,æplə'keʃən) n. 申請書

help (hɛlp) n. 〔美〕傭人

marketing ('morkitiŋ) n. 行銷（學）

apply for 申請

37. I have to brush up on my English.

Dialogue 1

A : Do you want to go to the movies tonight?
你今晚想去看電影嗎？

B : I can't. I have to brush up on my English.
我不能去。我得溫習英文。

A : Are you having a test tomorrow or something?
你明天有考試還是什麼？

B : Yes. We're having our mid-term.
是的。我們有期中考。

A : I wish you the best of luck.
我祝你好運。

B : Thanks. I'll need it.
謝謝。我需要它。

Dialogue 2

A : Do you have a driver's license?
你有駕照嗎？

B : No. I'm going to take the test in a couple of weeks.
沒有。我這幾週內就要去考。

A : Didn't you drive in your country?
你在你的國家不開車嗎？

B : Yes, but I have to brush up on driving.
開，但是我得溫習開車。

A : And you have to study the traffic rules, too.
　　而且你也得讀交通規則。

B : Right. There's a lot of new things I must learn.
　　對的，有很多新的事我必須學習。

Dialogue 3

A : I hear you're going to play the piano at the reception.
　　我聽說你在歡迎會上要彈鋼琴。

B : Yes. I'm kind of nervous.
　　是的，我有點緊張。

A : Nervous? You used to play very well.
　　緊張？你過去彈得很好。

B : But I haven't played for people in years.
　　但是我好幾年沒當衆彈了。

A : Oh, I guess you'll have to practice.
　　哦，我猜你得練習。

B : Yes, I have to brush up a little.
　　是的，我得溫習一下。

〔舉一反三〕

A : Are you busy tonight?
　　你今晚忙嗎？

B : Yes. I have to brush up on my English.
　　是的。我得溫習英文。

A : Did you study for the math test tomorrow?
　　明天的數學考試你讀了嗎？

B : Yes, but I have to brush up tonight, too.
　　是的，但是我今晚也得溫習。

A : Have you been practicing the violin?

　　你一直在練小提琴嗎？

B : No, I have to brush up a lot.

　　沒有，我得多溫習。

A : Are you free at 5 o'clock?

　　你五點有空嗎？

B : No, my class is having a meeting or something then.

　　沒空，我們班那時要開會或什麼的。

A : Doesn't Bob work in a bank?

　　鮑伯不是在銀行工作嗎？

B : Yes, I think he's a teller or something.

　　是的，我想他是出納員之類的。

【註釋】

brush up on 溫習

reception〔rɪ'sɛpʃən〕*n.* 歡迎會

kind of 有點

used to+**V.** 從前曾～

teller〔'tɛlɚ〕*n.*（銀行）出納員

38. *This milk has gone bad.*

Dialogue 1

A : Could I have a glass of milk?
　　我可以喝杯牛奶嗎？

B : Sure. I'll get you one.
　　當然。我給你拿一杯來。

A : Ooooh! This milk has gone bad.
　　嗯！這牛奶壞了。

B : Oh, I'm sorry. I just bought it a few days ago.
　　哦，對不起。我幾天前才買的。

A : Did you look at the stamp on the milk carton?
　　你有沒有看牛奶盒上的印記？

B : No, wait a minute. This carton is two weeks old.
　　沒有，等一下。這盒已經有兩個禮拜了！

Dialogue 2

A : Take a look at this bread.
　　瞧瞧這麵包。

B : It's stale.
　　這不新鮮。

A : Yes, it's hard as a rock.
　　是的，它硬得像石頭一樣。

B : Where did you buy it?
　　你在哪裏買的？

A : At the supermarket, just yesterday.
　　在超級市場，就是昨天。

B : You should take it back.
　　你該把它拿回去。

Dialogue 3

A : What's for lunch?
午餐吃什麼？

B : Well, I was going to make an omelette.
嗯，我本來要做煎蛋捲。

A : Why not, then?
後來爲什麼不做了？

B : I'm afraid the eggs are rotten.
我恐怕蛋是臭的。

A : Rotten? Why?
臭的？怎麼了？

B : I forgot to put them in the refrigerator.
我忘了把它們放進冰箱。

〔舉一反三〕

A : Can I help you, sir?
先生，我能爲你服務嗎？

B : Yes, this carton of milk has gone bad. I'd like to exchange it for a fresh one.
是的，這盒牛奶壞了。我想換盒新鮮的。

A : This beer is flat.
這啤酒走味了。

B : You should return it to the store.
你應該把它退還到店裏。

A : Waiter, this bread is stale.
侍者，這麵包不新鮮。

B : Oh, I'm terribly sorry. I'll get you a fresh piece.
噢，我很抱歉。我給你換新鮮的。

A : The hamburger meat has gone bad.

這漢堡肉壞了。

B : You should have put it in the freezer.

你本該把它放在冷凍庫的。

A : Waiter, this cream is sour.

侍者，這乳酪是酸的。。

B : Oh, I'm sorry. I'll get you some more.

哦，抱歉。我再拿些給你。

《 背景說明 》

　　go bad 可以籠統表示食物變壞，至於怎麼壞法，則要看所提到的食物是什麼了。譬如牛奶壞了，可用 This milk is *sour*. (變酸了) 或 This milk has *turned* (*sour*). 啤酒、可樂等飲料沒氣泡了、走味了，就說：This beer is *flat*. This coke is *flat*. 麵包不新鮮則說：This bread is *stale*. 蛋臭了，說：These eggs are *rotten*.

　　如果用 go bad 表示，則可說：This milk (or beer, coke, bread, egg, meat, food) *has gone bad*.

【註釋】

go bad 壞了　　stamp〔stæmp〕*n.* 戳記；標誌
carton〔'kartn〕*n.* 紙板盒
stale〔stel〕*adj.* 不新鮮的
omelette〔'amlɪt〕*n.* 煎蛋捲 (常以火腿、乳酪等作餡)
rotten〔'ratn〕*adj.* 臭的
flat〔flæt〕*adj.* 走味的
should have＋p.p. 表過去該做而未做的事
freezer〔'frizɚ〕*n.* 冷凍庫

39. *It doesn't make any difference.*

Dialogue 1

A : Shall I pick you up at 3 or 4?
　　我三點還是四點來接你？

B : It doesn't make any difference.
　　沒什麼差別。

A : O.K., I'll pick you up at 3.
　　好的，我三點去接你。

B : Fine.
　　好。

A : Shall we play tennis or golf on Sunday?
　　我們星期天要打網球還是高爾夫球？

B : It doesn't make any difference.
　　沒什麼差別。

Dialogue 2

A : Would you like to go to a play or a movie this evening?
　　今晚你想去看戲劇還是看電影？

B : It doesn't make any difference. Whichever you prefer.
　　沒什麼差別，看你喜歡什麼。

A : I enjoy them both, so I'd like you to make the choice.
　　我都喜歡，因此我想由你選擇。

B : That is very considerate of you. If you really feel that way, I'd prefer seeing a play.
　　你真體貼。如果你真覺得那樣，我想看戲劇。

A : Great. I'll pick up two tickets for the play at the Blackstone.

> 好極了。我會去買兩張黑石戲院戲劇的票。

B : Fine. I heard it's excellent.

> 好的。我聽說那戲劇非常好。

Dialogue 3

A : Jack, do you prefer blondes or brunettes?

> 傑克，你喜歡金髮女郎或是棕髮女郎？

B : I have no preference. I look at the girl, not her hair color.

> 我沒有偏好。我注意女孩本身，而不是她頭髮的顏色。

A : Don't you prefer one type over another?

> 你沒有比較喜歡哪一種嗎？

B : In some areas I do, but it's very difficult to say I like someone over someone else.

> 在某些方面是的，但是很難說我喜歡某人，甚於某人。

A : I think I understand what you're trying to say. You judge a girl by many qualities, not just one or two.

> 我想我了解你想要說什麼。你用很多特性來判斷女孩子，不只用一兩種。

B : Basically, that's right.

> 基本上那是對的。

〔舉一反三〕

A : Do you prefer apple or cherry pie?

> 你喜歡蘋果派還是櫻桃派？

B : I like them both.

> 我都喜歡。

A : Are you hoping for Dr. Greenberg or Dr. Little as your professor next year?

你希望明年格林柏格博士或列投博士作你的教授？

B : It doesn't matter to me.

我無所謂。

A : Which would you rather have, snowy weather or rain?

下雪或下雨天，你寧願要哪一種？

B : It's all the same to me.

對我來說都一樣。

A : Do you think we'll get a raise?

你認為我們會加薪嗎？

B : I don't know. I'd prefer better benefits.

我不知道。我寧願有更好的福利。

A : Would you care for a coke or a 7-up?

要來杯可樂還是汽水？

B : Either one will be fine.

都好。

【註釋】

pick up 買；得到

make a difference 有差別

make no difference 沒差別

blonde〔bland〕*n.* 有金黃色毛髮的人

brunette〔bruˈnɛt〕*n.* 髮、膚均為褐色的女子

40. I'm fed up with him.

Dialogue 1

A : Where's Bill? 比爾在哪裏？

B : Oh, he's probably at home with a hangover.
噢，他可能因昨晚酒醉不舒服，而待在家裏。

A : That's great! Now we have to do this work without him.
好極了！沒有他，我們自己做這工作。

B : Yes, this is the fourth time he's missed work this month.
是的，這是他這個月第四次忽略工作。

A : Even when he comes, he's too lazy to do very much.
即使他來，他也太懶了，做不了多少。

B : Right. I'm fed up with him.
對。我受夠他了。

Dialogue 2

A : Did you talk to your landlady yet?
你和你的女房東談過了嗎？

B : Yes, I've been calling her every day.
是的，我每天都打電話給她。

A : Is she going to fix the radiator, then?
那麼，她要修暖氣爐嗎？

B : Who knows? She never answers the phone.
誰知道？她從不接電話。

A : What are you going to do? 你要怎麼辦？

B : I don't know. I'm fed up with this apartment.
我不知道。我受夠了這公寓。

Dialogue 3

A：I hope I see you at Lucy's party.
我希望會在露西的宴會上看到你。

B：You won't. I decided not to go.
你看不到的。我決定不去。

A：Oh, you did? Is it because of Lucy's brother?
哦，你這麼決定了？是因為露西的哥哥嗎？

B：Sure, I've had it up to here with his passes.
當然是，我受夠了他的秋波。

A：You should really tell him you're not interested.
你真該告訴他，你沒興趣。

B：I did, and he still didn't stop.
我說了，但是他仍然不停止。

〔舉一反三〕

A：Your boss says you have to work late again.
你老板說你又得加班。

B：I'm fed up with him.
我受夠他了。

A：I'm sorry, we don't have any milk today.
對不起，我們今天沒有牛奶。

B：Not again! I'm fed up with this store.
又沒有！我受夠了這商店。

A：Do you have to pick your friend up from work?
你得從辦公室去接朋友嗎？

B：Yes, again. I'm fed up with going downtown every afternoon.
是的，又得去。我受夠了每天下午去市區。

A : Would you like to go out for dinner?
　　你想不想到外面吃晚飯？

B : Sure, I'm sick and tired of sitting at home.
　　當然，我厭倦了坐在家裏。

A : Mr. Jones said your paycheck will be late.
　　瓊斯先生說，你的薪水支票會晚一點。

B : I've had it up to here with this job.
　　我對這個工作受夠了。

《 背景説明 》

　　當一個人對某人或某件事物感到非常厭煩時，可以説：*I'm fed up with* ~. 或 *I have had it up to here with* ~. 這兩句原來是指吃得夠多或夠飽了。還可以加上手勢，將掌心朝下，水平放在脖子的位置，表示食物已塞滿到脖子了。後來由此意思引申為「受夠了~」。

　　一個愛喝酒的丈夫對妻子的嘮叨不耐煩時，可説：*I'm fed up with* my wife. She nags too much about my drinking. 一個對工作厭煩的員工常常會説：*I've had it up to* here with this lousy job.

　　另外一種表示厭煩的方法，就是 *I'm sick and tired of* it.

【註釋】

hangover (ˈhæŋˌovɚ) *n.* 宿醉
be fed up with = have had it up to here with 受夠~
landlady (ˈlændˌledɪ) *n.* 女房東
radiator (ˈredɪˌetɚ) *n.* 暖氣爐
pass〔pæs〕*n.* 秋波；媚眼
be sick and tired of 厭惡；厭倦
paycheck (ˈpeˈtʃɛk) *n.* 薪水支票（美國發薪水大都不發現金，發一張支票，這張支票就叫 paycheck。）

41. You can count on us.

Dialogue 1

A : Sue, can you drive Jane and me to the doctor on Monday?

蘇，你星期一可以開車載珍和我去看醫生嗎？

B : I think so.

我想可以。

A : We need a ride very badly. Are you sure you'll be able to help out?

我們迫切需要乘車。你確定能協助嗎？

B : Sure. I'll mark it on my calendar so I don't forget.

當然。我會在月曆上做記號，那麼就不會忘了。

A : Thanks. You're a good friend.

謝謝。你是個好朋友。

B : You can always count on me when you need help.

你需要幫助的時候，可以指望我。

Dialogue 2

A : Mary, you will be coming to our club meeting, won't you?

瑪莉，你會來我們俱樂部的聚會吧，是不？

B : Of course. I haven't forgotten.

當然，我沒忘記。

A : I've one request. Can you bring your slides of Mexico?

我有個請求。你能帶你墨西哥的幻燈片嗎？

B : Certainly. Do you have a projector?

當然。你有放映機嗎？

A : Yes, everything will be set up. We'll be counting on you.

是的，一切都會弄好。我們要靠你了。

B : Fine. I'm always happy to show my slides.

好的。我一向很高興放我的幻燈片。

Dialogue 3

A : I'd like some help when I move next week.

下週我搬家的時候，需要一些幫助。

B : You can count on me.

你可以依賴我。

A : Thanks. I'll have to ask a couple more people.

謝謝。我還得再找幾個人。

B : My brother can help out.

我弟弟可以幫忙。

A : Good. Can your friend Jim come, too?

好的。你的朋友吉姆也能來嗎？

B : I don't think so. You can't count on him for anything.

我想不能。你任何事都不能指望他。

〔舉一反三〕

A : Will you and your wife be able to come?

你和你太太能來嗎？

B : Sure. You can count on us.

當然，你可以相信我們。

A : Can I count on you to bring refreshments?

我能指望你帶點心來嗎？

B : Yes, I'll be sure to bring some.

是的，我一定會帶一些來。

A : I can drive you downtown tomorrow.

我明天可以開車載你去市中心。

B : Thanks. I'll be counting on you.

謝謝。我就靠你了。

A : We need you at the meeting very badly.

我們極需要你出席會議。

B : OK. Count on me.

好的,相信我。

A : Do you think Susan can help out?

你想蘇珊能幫忙嗎?

B : No, you can't count on her.

不,你不能指望她。

【註釋】

Sue〔su〕*n.* 女子名(Susan, Susanna 的暱稱)

help out 協助   *count on* 依賴;指望

slide〔slaɪd〕*n.* 幻燈片

projector〔prə'dʒɛktə〕*n.* 放映機

a couple(*of*) 幾個;一對(美國口語中有時省略 of)

42. *I'd like a refund.*

Dialogue 1

A : Excuse me, Ma'am.
　　對不起，女士。

B : Yes, can I help you?
　　是的，我能為你服務嗎？

A : Yes, I bought this toaster here yesterday, but it doesn't work.
　　是的，我昨天在這裏買了這個烤麵包機，但是它不能用。

B : Do you have a receipt?
　　你有收據嗎？

A : Yes, I do. I'd like a refund.
　　是的，我有。我想退錢。

B : All right. I'll see what I can do.
　　好的。我看看該怎麼辦。

Dialogue 2

A : Can I have a refund on this sweater?
　　這件毛線衣我能退錢嗎？

B : No, I'm afraid we can't do that.
　　不，我恐怕我們不能退。

A : Well, then can I exchange it for another one?
　　好吧，那麼我可以換另一件嗎？

B : Yes, of course.
　　是的，當然。

A : I think I'd like that brown turtleneck.
我想我要那件咖啡色的套頭高領毛衣。

B : All right. Let me wrap it for you.
好的。我包給你。

Dialogue 3

A : I have a complaint.
我有句怨言。

B : Yes, sir. What's the problem?
是的,先生。有什麼問題?

A : You sold me these shoes a week ago. Well, the heels fell off after two days.
你一星期以前賣給我這鞋子。嗯,兩天後,鞋後跟就掉了。

B : I'm terribly sorry about that.
關於那件事我非常抱歉。

A : So am I. I want my money back.
我也是。我要退錢。

B : I'm afraid we can't give refunds.
恐怕我們不能退錢。

〔舉一反三〕

A : I'd like a refund on this blender.
我要退這攪拌器的錢。

B : You'll have to see the manager.
你得去見經理。

A : I'd like my money back.
我要退錢。

B : Do you have a sales slip?
你有發票嗎?

A : This mixer doesn't work. I want a refund.
　　這攪拌器不會動。我要退錢。

B : I'm afraid the store doesn't give refunds.
　　恐怕這個店不退錢。

A : Can I have my money back on this jacket?
　　我可以退這件夾克的錢嗎？

B : No, but you can exchange it for another one.
　　不可以，但是你可以換另外一件。

A : I'd like to exchange this vacuum cleaner.
　　我想換這真空吸塵器。

B : Certainly. Can I see the receipt?
　　當然。我可以看收據嗎？

【註釋】

ma'am〔mæm,mɑm〕n. 女士；太太（= madam）

toaster〔'tostə〕n. 烤麵包機　　receipt〔rɪ'sit〕n. 收據

refund〔'ri,fʌnd〕n. 退錢

turtleneck〔'tɝtḷ,nɛk〕n. 有翻折高領的毛線衣

heel〔hil〕n. 鞋後跟　　blender〔'blɛndə〕n. 攪拌器

sales slip 銷貨傳票；發票　　mixer〔'mɪksə〕n. 攪拌器

vacuum〔'vækjuəm〕n. 真空　　*vacuum cleaner* 真空吸塵器

43. *It doesn't work.*

Dialogue 1

A : You're not wearing your new watch.
　　你沒戴你的新錶。

B : No, it doesn't work.
　　沒有，它不走了。

A : Doesn't work? But you got it only a month ago.
　　不走？但是你一個月前才買的。

B : They don't make them like they used to.
　　他們做錶不像以前那樣。

A : Do you know what's wrong with it?
　　你知道它有什麼毛病嗎？

B : I think the mainspring is broken.
　　我想主發條斷了。

Dialogue 2

A : Can you take a look at my tape recorder? It isn't working.
　　你看看我的錄音機好嗎？它不動了。

B : What's the problem? 有什麼毛病？

A : I push the "play" button and nothing happens.
　　我按「放」鈕，但是沒結果。

B : Hmmm... did you check the batteries?
　　嗯……你檢查了電池嗎？

A : Oh, no! I bet the batteries are dead.
　　哦，沒有！我敢說是電池沒電了。

B : Then that's your problem.
　　那麼就是你的問題了。

Dialogue 3

A : Why are you so tired?
　　你爲什麼那麼累？

B : I had to walk up five flights of stairs.
　　我得走上五層樓的樓梯。

A : Why didn't you use the elevator?
　　你爲什麼不用電梯？

B : It was out of order.
　　它故障了。

A : Not again! That elevator breaks down about once a week.
　　別再故態又犯，那電梯大約一週故障一次。

B : They ought to fix it.
　　他們應該修的。

〔舉一反三〕

A : Did you hear that news today?
　　你今天聽新聞了嗎？

B : No, my radio doesn't work.
　　沒有，我的收音機壞了。

A : Why don't we eat dinner at your house?
　　我們何不在你家吃晚飯？

B : We can't. My stove isn't working.
　　我們不行。我的爐子壞了。

A : Is your television still broken?
　　你的電視機還是壞的嗎？

B : Yes. I had it fixed twice, and it still doesn't work.
　　是的。我叫人修過兩次了，可是還是壞的。

A : Why are all these cars lined up on the street?
　　這些車子為什麼都排在街上？
B : The traffic light is out of order.
　　紅綠燈故障了。

A : I lost 30 cents in that pay phone.
　　我在那公用電話損失了三毛。
B : Didn't you see the sign? It's out of order.
　　你沒看到那標誌嗎？它故障了。

━━

【註釋】

It doesn't work. 它不動了。
It's out of order. = **It breaks down.** 它故障了。
mainspring〔'men,sprɪŋ〕 *n.* （使鐘錶轉動的）主發條
tape recorder 錄音機
battery〔'bætərɪ〕 *n.* 電池
I bet 我敢說；我相信

44. It's better than nothing.

Dialogue 1

A : I put a dollar in the change machine, but I only got 95 cents back.
我把一塊錢放到換零錢的機器裏，但是只拿回了九毛五分。

B : Oh, well, it's better than nothing.
嗯，總比什麼都沒有好。

A : No, it isn't. I got short-changed!
不，不是這麼說。我給少找錢了。

B : Are you going to ask for your money back?
你要討回你的錢嗎？

A : Sure. Who should I talk to?
當然。我該和誰談？

B : You have to see the manager.
你得去見經理。

Dialogue 2

A : Did you ask Mr. Thompson for a raise?
你向湯普生先生要求加薪了嗎？

B : Yes, I asked for 50 cents an hour more.
是的，我要求一小時加五毛錢。

A : Did you get it?
你如願以償了嗎？

B : No, I got 25 cents.
沒有，我只加了兩毛五分。

A : That's too bad. 那眞可惜。

B : Oh, it's all right. It's better than nothing.
哦，那還好。總比一毛都沒有好。

Dialogue 3

A : When are you taking your vacation?
你什麼時候休假?

B : Next month. I'll be gone for ten days.
下個月。我要休十天。

A : Ten days? I thought you were going for two weeks.
十天?我以為你要休兩個星期呢!

B : I was, but then I realized I can't afford to be gone for so long.
我本來是的,但是我後來了解到,我去不起那麼久。

A : I guess ten days is better than nothing.
我想十天總比一天都沒有好。

B : Yes, I might as well go for as long as I can.
是的,我還是盡我所能,休得久一點。

〔舉一反三〕

A : Did you get the day off?
你那天休假了嗎?

B : No, just the afternoon. But it's better than nothing.
沒有,只是下午。但比什麼都沒有要好。

A : Will we have steak for dinner?
我們晚餐吃牛排嗎?

B : No, only hamburger. But it's better than nothing.
不,只有漢堡。但總比什麼都沒有要好。

A : I don't have fifty cents, but I can give you a quarter.
我沒有五毛錢,但是我可以給你兩毛五分。

B : O.K. That's better than nothing.
好的。那比一毛也沒要好。

A : Did the cashier give you the correct change?
　　出納員找給你的零錢對嗎？

B : No, she didn't. I got short-changed.
　　不，她找得不對。我給少找錢了。

A : There aren't any more tickets for the play.
　　這齣戲沒有多餘的票了。

B : Then we might as well go to a movie.
　　那麼我們還是去看電影吧。

《背景說明》

　　所獲得的東西比預期的少，仍覺得滿足，則可說：*It's better than nothing*. 因此無論是少找了錢、加薪加太少、休假休太少、餐飲不夠豐盛、…等等，只要不嫌棄，就可用這句話。

　　有句常見的諺語也表示類似的意義：Half a loaf is better than no bread.「半條麵包總比沒有麵包好；聊勝於無。」

【註釋】

short-change (ˌʃɔrt'tʃendʒ) *vt.* 少找錢；找錢不足
might as well + V. 不妨；不也可以；還是
quarter ('kwɔrtɚ) *n.* 二角五分之硬幣
cashier (kæ'ʃɪr) *n.* 出納員

45. Drop me off at the Hilton.

Dialogue 1

A : Jane, are you going shopping?
珍，妳要去逛街嗎？

B : Yes. I'm going after breakfast.
是的。我早餐後要去逛街。

A : Could you drop me off somewhere?
你可以載我到某個地方嗎？

B : Where do you want to go?
妳想去哪裡？

A : I need a ride to the Hilton.
我得坐車去希爾頓。

B : Sure. It's on my way.
好的。那順路。

Dialogue 2

A : Hi, Tracy. 嗨，崔西。

B : Hi, Bill. 嗨，比爾。

A : I haven't seen you for a long time.
我好久沒看到妳了。

B : Right. I took a year off from school. I'm headed for the admissions office now.
是的。我休學了一年。現在我要去入學許可辦公室。

A : Can I drop you off? I'm going that way.
要我載你一程嗎？我走那條路。

B : Yes, thanks for the lift.
好的，謝謝你讓我搭便車。

Dialogue 3

A : Jane, are you going into Chicago today?
珍，你今天要進芝加哥嗎？

B : No, I'm not. Why?
沒有，我沒有要去。什麼事？

A : I have to run an errand for Jack.
我得幫傑克跑腿。

B : I can take you in tomorrow.
我可以明天帶你去。

A : Fine. Would you drop me off at Wilson and Broadway?
好的。你載我到威爾遜街和百老匯的交口好嗎？

B : Sure. Maybe we can have lunch together.
當然。或許我們可以一起吃中飯。

〔舉一反三〕

A : Can you drop me off at the bank?
你能載我到那家銀行嗎？

B : Sure. I'm leaving in a minute.
當然。我馬上就走。

A : Do you need a lift?
你需要搭便車嗎？

B : Yes. Can you drop me off at the grocery store?
是的。你能載我到雜貨店嗎？

A : Jack needs a ride home.
傑克得搭車回家。

B : I'll take him.
我載他。

A : Do you need a ride?

　　你需要坐車嗎？

B : No, thanks. I have my own car.

　　不用，謝謝。我自己有車。

A : Can I drop you somewhere?

　　要我載你到什麼地方嗎？

B : No, thanks. I have a ride.

　　不用了，謝謝你。有人載我。

【註釋】

drop〔drɑp〕*vt.* 使（人或物）離開車、船

drop sb. off 讓某人下車

be headed for 前往～

admission〔əd'mɪʃən〕*n.* 許可

lift〔lɪft〕*n.* 搭便車

run an errand 跑腿

Sure. It's on my way.

I need a ride to the Hilton.

46. *Think nothing of it.*

Dialogue 1

A : Oh no, I don't have my wallet.
哦不，我的皮夾不見了。

B : You're sure you didn't leave it in the room?
你確定你沒把它留在房間裏嗎？

A : I'm sure. And I promised to buy dinner.
我確定。而且我答應要付晚餐的。

B : Don't worry about that. I'll pick up the check.
別擔心。我會去付帳。

A : Thanks. I'll pay you back later.
謝謝。我以後會還你。

B : Think nothing of it.
別掛記它。

Dialogue 2

A : Did you wear my tie to the dance, Bill?
比爾，你戴我的領帶去舞會了嗎？

B : Yes, but I'm afraid I had a little accident.
是的，但是我恐怕有了點小意外。

A : What happened?
怎麼回事？

B : I spilled beer on it. I'm really sorry.
我把啤酒灑在上面了。我真抱歉。

A : That's O.K., think nothing of it.
沒關係，別掛記它。

B : You're a real pal. I'll have it cleaned for you.
你真夠朋友。我會為你洗乾淨的。

Dialogue 3

A : Did you go shopping this afternoon?
　　你今天下午去逛街了嗎?

B : Yes, and I bought the things you wanted.
　　是的,而且我買了你要的東西。

A : Did you get me a typewriter ribbon?
　　你給我買了打字機的色帶嗎?

B : Yes, but I think it's the wrong size.
　　買了,但是我想尺寸錯了。

A : That's all right. Think nothing of it.
　　沒關係。別掛記它。

B : Maybe I can exchange it tomorrow.
　　或許我明天可以去換。

〔舉一反三〕

A : You're doing me a big favor, Fred.
　　傅萊德,你幫了我一個大忙。

B : It's O.K. Think nothing of it.
　　沒什麼。別放在心上。

A : I forgot to mail your letter.
　　我忘了寄你的信。

B : Think nothing of it. I'll mail it tomorrow.
　　別放在心上。我明天寄。

A : Thanks for a wonderful meal, Gladys.
　　格萊蒂絲,謝謝豐盛的一頓。

B : Think nothing of it. We enjoy having you.
　　別放在心上。我們喜歡和你在一起。

A： I'm sorry I forgot to call you last night.
抱歉我昨晚忘了打電話給你。

B： Think nothing of it. I wasn't home, anyway.
別放在心上。反正我不在家。

A： I'll have to borrow some money.
我得借些錢。

B： That's O.K. You can pay me back later.
沒關係。你可以以後還我。

【註釋】

think nothing of 輕視；認為無所謂
spill〔spɪl〕*vt.* 灑
pal〔pæl〕*n.* 朋友
ribbon〔'rɪbən〕*n.* 色帶；緞帶
Gladys〔'glædɪs〕*n.* 格萊蒂絲（女子名）

47. *The same to you*.

Dialogue 1

A : I'm exhausted.
我筋疲力盡了。

B : How come?
爲什麼？

A : I typed thirty letters today. I'm going to go home and sleep.
我今天打了三十封信。我要回家睡覺了。

B : Yeah, I'm tired, too.
是的，我也累了。

A : Well, have a nice weekend.
嗯，週末愉快。

B : O.K., same to you.
好的，你也一樣。

Dialogue 2

A : I'm going for an important job interview tomorrow.
我明天要去一個重要的工作面談。

B : Oh, really? Are you nervous?
哦，眞的？你緊張嗎？

A : Sure, a little. Don't you have an interview next week?
當然有一點。你下週不是有個面談嗎？

B : Yes, it's for a much better-paying job.
是的，是個待遇好得多的工作。

A : Well, I hope you have good luck.

嗯，我祝你好運。

B : And the same to you.

你也一樣。

Dialogue 3

A : I think Mike's a real dummy.

我認為邁克眞是個傻瓜。

B : Oh? Why do you say that?

哦？你爲什麼那麼說？

A : The way he screwed up that job.

他把那工作搞得一團糟的樣子。

B : No, I don't agree. He did what he had to do.

不，我不同意。他做了他該做的。

A : Oh yeah? Well, then you're dumber than he is.

哦，是嗎？嗯，那你比他還笨。

B : Oh yeah? Well, the same goes for you.

哦，是嗎？嗯，那你也一樣。

〔舉一反三〕

A : Have a nice weekend.

週末愉快。

B : Thank you. Same to you.

謝謝你。你也一樣。

A : Have a nice vacation.

假期愉快。

B : Thank you. You, too.

謝謝你。你也一樣。

A : Good luck on your test tomorrow.
　　祝你明天考試好運。

B : And the same to you.
　　你也一樣。

A : Merry Christmas.
　　聖誕快樂。

B : Same to you.
　　你也一樣。

A : I think Jim is very lazy.
　　我認為吉姆很懶。

B : And the same goes for his brother, too.
　　他的哥哥也一樣。

《背景說明》

碰到別人祝福我們的時候，通常都要有禮貌地回答：**The same to you**.「你也一樣。」這類的祝福有：Have a nice trip (or weekend, holiday, vacation, time,……). Good luck on your test tomorrow. 或是固定節日的祝福語，如：Merry Christmas！Happy New Year.

有時候簡單的回答是 Thank you. **You too**. 但限於較熟悉的朋友。

【註釋】

exhausted〔ɪgˋzɔstɪd〕adj. 筋疲力竭的
How come? 為什麼？
Mike〔maɪk〕n. 邁克（男子名）
dummy〔ˋdʌmɪ〕n. 傻瓜　　**screw up** 弄糟
dumb〔dʌm〕adj.〔美俗〕愚笨的

48. *I can't stand it.*

Dialogue 1

A : How's your new apartment?
你的新的公寓怎樣？

B : I thought it was in a quiet neighborhood, but it isn't.
我以爲它四周很安靜，但是並非如此。

A : What's the problem?
有什麼問題？

B : One of my neighbors has a dog.
我的一位鄰居有狗。

A : Does it make a lot of noise?
牠製造很多噪音嗎？

B : It barks all night long. I can't stand it.
牠整晚都叫。我受不了。

Dialogue 2

A : I hope Marie isn't here.
我希望瑪莉不在這裏。

B : Why?
爲什麼？

A : Because Bob is coming over soon.
因爲鮑伯馬上要來。

B : Isn't Bob always asking Marie for a date?
鮑伯不是老是邀瑪莉出去嗎？

A : That's right. But Marie can't stand him.
對的。但是瑪莉受不了他。

B : Poor Bob. He doesn't know when to quit.
可憐的鮑伯。他不知道適時停止。

Dialogue 3

A : What happened to Janet?
　　珍妮特怎麼了？

B : She left her job at the advertising company.
　　她離開廣告公司的工作。

A : Why？ I thought she was making good money.
　　為什麼？我以為她正賺大錢。

B : She was, but she couldn't take it anymore.
　　她是的，但是她沒辦法再忍受。

A : Take what？
　　忍受什麼？

B : The hours. She was working up to 60 hours a week.
　　工作時數。她一週要工作到六十小時。

〔舉一反三〕

A : Do you like the weather here？
　　你喜歡這裏的天氣嗎？

B : No, I can't stand it. It's too hot.
　　不，我不能忍受它。它太熱了。

A : Does Bill enjoy visiting your relatives？
　　比爾喜歡拜訪你的親戚嗎？

B : No, he can't stand them.
　　不，他受不了他們。

A : Why did you quit your job？
　　你為什麼辭職？

B : I couldn't take it anymore.
　　我沒辦法再忍受下去。

A : The music in that restaurant is too loud.

那家餐廳的音樂太大聲了。

B : Yes, it's too much to take.

是的，大聲到難以忍受。

A : Jim usually drinks too much at parties.

吉姆在宴會中通常喝得太多。

B : Right. He doesn't know when to quit.

對的。他不知道什麼時候該停止。

【註釋】

stand〔stænd〕*vt.* 忍受

Marie〔ˈmɑrɪ, ˈmærɪ〕*n.* 瑪莉（女子名）

too ~ to 太～以致於不

One of my neighbors has a dog.

It barks all night long. I can't stand it.

49. I'm not myself today.

Dialogue 1

A : We had a meeting at 10 o'clock. Where were you?
我們十點有集會。你在哪裏?

B : I'm sorry. I guess I forgot.
抱歉,我想我忘了。

A : Forgot? How could you forget?
忘了?你怎麼能忘呢?

B : I don't know. I'm not myself today.
我不知道。我今天心神不定。

A : What's wrong?
怎麼了?

B : Maybe I'm just tired. I haven't been getting much sleep.
或許我只是累了。我一直睡得不夠。

Dialogue 2

A : I'm not feeling like myself today.
我今天有點失常。

B : Why? You look well enough.
怎麼了?你看起來很好。

A : Yes, but I'm worried about things.
是的,但是我在擔心事情。

B : What things?
什麼事?

A : Well, lots of things. For one, my wife's in the hospital again.

嗯，很多事。其中之一，我太太又住院了。

B : That's too bad. I hope she's better soon.

那真不幸。我希望她很快康復。

Dialogue 3

A : Did you hear Gordon arguing with Irene?

你聽說了戈登和愛琳爭吵嗎？

B : Yes. I don't think Gordon's himself today.

聽說了。我認爲戈登今天有點失常。

A : I wonder what's the matter with him.

我想知道他有什麼問題。

B : Perhaps he's just over-worked.

或許他只是工作過度了。

A : But he shouldn't yell at Irene.

但是他不該對愛琳咆哮。

B : Right. She's been under the weather herself.

對。愛琳一直身體不舒服。

〔舉一反三〕

A : You weren't paying attention in class today.

你今天在課堂上不專心。

B : I know. I'm not myself today.

我知道。我今天心神不定。

A : Jim was rather upset when I saw him.

我看到吉姆的時候，他很難過。

B : Don't worry. He's not himself today.

別擔心。他今天失常。

A : Mrs. Parker isn't feeling herself today.
　　派克太太今天有點失常。

B : Maybe she's got the flu.
　　或許她得了流行性感冒。

A : Do you want to go out to dinner tonight?
　　你今晚想出去吃晚飯嗎?

B : No, thanks. I'm feeling under the weather.
　　不,謝了。我覺得不舒服。

A : I don't feel up to par this afternoon.
　　我今天下午覺得不舒服。

B : No, you don't look well.
　　對的,你臉色不太好。

┌─ 《 背景説明 》 ─┐

　　I'm not myself. 可以表示心神上的不寧,以及身體上的不適,但用於前者的情形較多。如别人問你 What's the matter with you? 可回答:My father had a heart attack last night and he is in the hospital. *I'm not myself today.* 以表示心神不寧。

　　如果是身體上的不適,通常用 *I'm under the weather.* 或 I don't *feel well.* 因此,身體不舒服,可以説:I'm feeling a little *under the weather* today, so I'd like to go home early.

【註釋】

be oneself 頭腦(身體)正常
Gordon 〔'gɔrdn̩〕 n. 戈登(男子名)
Irene 〔aɪ'rin〕 n. 愛琳(女子名)
yell 〔jɛl〕 vi. 咆哮　　*under the weather* 病的;身體不適的
upset 〔ʌp'sɛt〕 adj. 難過的　　*up to par* 合乎正常狀態

50. *I hope you saved room for dessert.*

Dialogue 1

A : I hope you enjoyed your meal.
我希望你這頓飯吃得愉快。

B : Yes, it was delicious. 是的，味道很好。

A : Thank you. I hope you saved room for dessert. I have a fresh apple pie.
謝謝你。我希望你留了點肚子吃甜點。我有新鮮的蘋果派。

B : I'm full, but that sounds too good to pass up.
我飽了，但是那似乎太棒了，讓我無法拒絕。

A : Would you like to wait a little before having dessert?
你吃甜點前要不要等一下？

B : Yes, if you don't mind. 好的，如果你不介意的話。

Dialogue 2

A : The meal was delicious. You're an excellent cook.
這頓飯很好吃。你是個最棒的廚師。

B : Thank you for the compliment. Are you ready for dessert? 謝謝你的恭維。你準備好吃甜點了嗎？

A : Certainly. What are we having?
當然。我們吃什麼？

B : Fresh blueberry pie with lots of whipped cream.
新鮮的藍莓派，加了很多泡沫鮮奶油。

A : How did you know that blueberry pie is my favorite?
你怎麼知道我最喜歡吃藍莓派？

B : I didn't, but since I guessed right, I hope you'll have room for a second serving.
我不知道，但是既然我猜對了，希望你吃得下第二份。

Dialogue 3

A : Did you save some room for Kathy?
你給凱西留了位子嗎？

B : Yes. She can sit next to Jane.
是的，她可以坐在珍旁邊。

A : How many people can we get into this car?
這輛車能坐幾個人？

B : Six. Seven if we squeeze a little.
六個。如果我們擠一點，可以坐七個。

A : It's a long ride to the picnic grounds. I think we should only take six.
到野餐的地方還要開很久，我想我們坐六個就好。

B : I guess you're right.
我想你是對的。

〔舉一反三〕

A : Did you save room for dessert?
你留了肚子吃甜點嗎？

B : I always have room for dessert.
我總是有肚子吃甜點。

A : Did you schedule some time for a tennis game?
你有沒有安排一些時間打一場網球？

B : Sure. I saved an hour just for you.
當然。我為你留了一個鐘頭。

A : If you can go tomorrow, I'll save some room in the car for you.
如果你明天能去，我會在車裡留你的位子。

B : I'll let you know tonight.
我今晚會告訴你。

A : I hope everyone saved room for ice cream.

　　　我希望每個人都留了肚子吃冰淇淋。

B : I'll have two servings.

　　　我要吃兩份。

A : Don't eat too much bread. Save room for the main course.

　　　別吃太多麵包。留點肚子吃主菜。

B : I can't help it. I'm hungry.

　　　我沒辦法。我餓了。

《 背景説明 》

　　一般人都知道 *room* 的意思是「房間」，這時的 room 是個可數名詞，例如你到旅館去問有沒有空房間，就可以説：Do you have *a room* for tonight？

　　room 也常作「空間、餘地」，意思相當於 space。飯後問別人還吃不吃得下甜點，就説：Do you have *room* for dessert？

　　搭車的時候，詢問還有沒有空位，可説：Do you have enough *room*？或 Is there *room* for me in this car？回答：We'll move over and *make room for* you.

【註釋】

dessert〔dɪˈzɜt〕*n.* 餐後用的甜點心　　*pass up* 放棄；拒絕

compliment〔ˈkɑmpləmənt〕*n.* 恭維

blueberry〔ˈbluˌbɛrɪ,-bərɪ〕*n.* 越橘屬的漿果；藍莓

whipped〔hwɪpt〕*adj.* 攪成泡沫狀的

serving〔ˈsɜvɪŋ〕*n.*（點心、飯菜等）一人份；一客

squeeze〔skwiz〕*vi.* 擠；壓縮

schedule〔ˈskɛdʒul〕*vt.* 排定（在某時間做某事）　　*main course* 主菜

51. I'd like to ask for a raise.

Dialogue 1

A : Mr. Gardner, may I see you for a moment?

　　葛德納先生，我可不可以見你一會兒？

B : Sure, Mr. Yi. Come in and sit down.

　　當然，易先生。進來坐。

A : Thank you.

　　謝謝你。

B : What can I do for you?

　　要我爲你做什麼？

A : Well, I've been working here for nine months and I feel I deserve a raise.

　　我在這裡已經做了九個月，我覺得我應該加薪了。

B : Let me give it some thought.

　　我考慮一下。

Dialogue 2

A : What can I do for you, Jim?

　　吉姆，要我爲你做什麼？

B : Mr. Brown, you know, the rate of inflation is so high, it's getting difficult to make ends meet. I need a raise.

　　布朗先生，你知道，通貨膨脹率一直這麼高，要收支平衡愈來愈難。我需要加薪。

A : I understand, Jim. When was the last time you got a raise?

　　我了解的，吉姆。你上次加薪是什麼時候？

B : Fifteen months ago.

　　十五個月以前。

A : O.K., I'll speak to the bookkeeper about a raise for you.
　　好的。我會對會計說加你的薪。

B : Thank you very much, Mr. Brown.
　　非常感謝你，布朗先生。

Dialogue 3

A : What are you doing, Bob?
　　鮑伯，你在做什麼？

B : I'm practicing my speech.
　　我正在練習演說。

A : What speech?
　　什麼演說？

B : I'm going to ask for a raise.
　　我將要求加薪。

A : Why do you have to practice?
　　你為什麼需要練習？

B : Because I'm nervous.
　　因為我很緊張。

〔舉一反三〕

A : I'd like to ask for a raise, sir.
　　先生，我想要求加薪。

B : Do you feel you deserve it?
　　你覺得你應該加嗎？

A : I'd like to ask for a raise, but I don't have the nerve to do it.
　　我想要求加薪，但是我沒有勇氣那麼做。

B : Why not?
　　為什麼沒有？

A : After seven years with the company, sir, I feel I deserve more money.

先生，我在這公司做了七年，我認為我應得更多的錢。

B : I agree with you, Bill.

我同意你，比爾。

A : I'd like to have a pay raise.

我想要加薪。

B : Why?

為什麼？

A : When am I entitled to a raise?

我什麼時候有資格加薪？

B : After 6 months with the company.

在這公司六個月以後。

【註釋】

deserve〔dɪ'zɝv〕*vt.* 應得

raise〔rez〕*n.* (待遇等之) 提高；加薪

inflation〔ɪn'fleʃən〕*n.* 通貨膨脹

make ends meet 收支平衡

bookkeeper〔'bʊk,kipɚ〕*n.* 會計員；記帳員

nerve〔nɝv〕*n.* 勇氣

entitle〔ɪn'taɪtl̩〕*vt.* 使有資格

52. *Give me a ballpark figure*.

Dialogue 1

A : How much did you pay for your stereo?
你買音響花了多少錢？

B : Oh! I don't remember. It was so long ago.
哦！我不記得了。那麼久以前的事。

A : Can you give me a ballpark figure?
你可不可以給我一個大概的數目？

B : Roughly, I'd say around 40,000 dollars.
大約四萬元左右。

A : Do you have any idea how much it costs now?
你知不知道現在要多少錢？

B : I can only give you a ballpark figure. I'd say
around 60,000.
我只能給你一個大概的數目。大約六萬元。

Dialogue 2

A : How much money do you think Jack would want
in order to work for us?
你認為傑克為我們工作會要多少薪水？

B : I really don't know.
我真的不知道。

A : Can you give me a ballpark figure?
你可以給我一個大概的數字嗎？

B : I'd say between 25,000 and 30,000 dollars.
兩萬五到三萬吧。

A : Ask him to come in and discuss it with me.
　　要他來和我談談。

B : I'll call him today.
　　我今天會打電話給他。

Dialogue 3

A : What do you want for your car?
　　你的車要賣多少錢？

B : I've never thought about it.
　　我從沒想過。

A : Can you give me an estimate?
　　你能告訴我估計的價錢嗎？

B : Probably around 150,000 dollars.
　　大約十五萬吧。

A : That sounds fair.
　　似乎很公道。

B : Are you seriously interested?
　　你眞的感興趣嗎？

〔舉一反三〕

A : Can you give me a ballpark figure?
　　你能給我一個大槪的數字嗎？

B : I'd say around 2,500 dollars.
　　大約兩千五百元。

A : Do you think 15,500 dollars would be in the ball-
　　park?
　　你認爲一萬五千元還算可以嗎？

B : That sounds good.
　　似乎很好。

A : Do you know if 200 dollars would be in the ballpark?
　　你認爲兩百元還算可以嗎？

B : I think you're a little low.
　　我認爲太低了點。

A : How many people showed up for the meeting?
　　多少人出席那項會議？

B : Do you want the ballpark figure?
　　你要大概的數字嗎？

A : How much would it cost to fix my car?
　　我的車修理要多少錢？

B : Three thousand dollars would be a fair estimate.
　　三千元是合理的估計。

《背景説明》

　　ballpark 的原意是「棒球場」，引申的意思是「大約的；還算可以的」。
a ballpark figure（大約的數字），相當於 *approximation* 。

　　當你求職應徵時，主事者可能會問你希望的待遇大約是多少：
What kind of salary were you thinking of? You can give
me *a ballpark figure*.

　　當你要買賣東西，問別人出的價錢還可以嗎，就説：Do you think
X dollars would be *in the ballpark*？

【註釋】

stereo (ˈstɛrɪo, ˈstɪrɪo) *n.* 立體音響設備
ballpark (ˈbɔlˌpɑrk) *adj.* 大約的　　roughly (ˈrʌflɪ) *adv.* 大約地
estimate (ˈɛstəmɪt) *n.* 估計　　*show up* 出現

53. Don't mention it.

Dialogue 1

A : I'm sorry I stepped on your toe.
我很抱歉踩到你的腳趾。

B : It's O.K. Don't mention it.
沒關係，別提了。

A : Are you sure you're O.K.?
你確定沒事嗎？

B : Yes, I'm fine. Thank you.
是的，我很好。謝謝你。

A : I hope you're enjoying the party.
我希望你舞會玩得愉快。

B : Yes, it's a nice party.
是的，這是個愉快的舞會。

Dialogue 2

A : Thanks for helping me last night.
謝謝你昨晚幫我忙。

B : Don't mention it.
不客氣。

A : You're a good friend.
你真是個好朋友。

B : I'm glad you feel that way.
我很高興你那麼想。

A : I hope I can repay the favor soon.
我希望很快能報答你。

B : Don't worry about it.
別擔心。

Dialogue 3

A : May I use your telephone?
　　我能借用你的電話嗎？

B : Sure. It's in the living room.
　　當然。電話在客廳裡。

A : Thank you.
　　謝謝你。

B : You're welcome.
　　不客氣。

A : I'm sorry to be such a pest.
　　抱歉這麼麻煩你。

B : No problem.
　　沒關係。

〔 舉一反三 〕

A : Thanks for the help.
　　謝謝你幫忙。

B : Don't mention it.
　　不客氣。

A : I'm glad you came.
　　我很高興你來了。

B : Don't mention it.
　　不客氣。

A : Thanks for helping us.
　　謝謝你幫我們。

B : Think nothing of it.
　　別放在心上。

A : I tried to find you a job, but it didn't work out.
　　我試著幫你找工作，但是沒找成。

B : That's all right.
　　沒關係。

A : Thank you for taking care of James for me.
　　謝謝你幫我照顧詹姆斯。

B : Don't mention it.
　　別客氣。

【註釋】

repay〔rɪ'pe〕*vt.* 報答
favor〔'fevɚ〕*n.* 恩惠
pest〔pɛst〕*n.* 令人討厭的人或物
think nothing of 認為～無所謂
living room 客廳

54. Your tie looks good on you.

Dialogue 1

A : Your tie looks good on you.
你打這條領帶很好看。

B : Thank you. It's nice of you to say so.
謝謝你。你這麼說真好。

A : Where did you get it?
你的領帶哪裡買的?

B : My sister gave it to me.
我姊姊給我的。

A : It goes well with your suit.
它和你這套衣服很配。

B : Thank you.
謝謝你。

Dialogue 2

A : What do you think of this hat?
你認為這頂帽子如何?

B : It looks good on you.
你戴起來很好看。

A : What about the color?
顏色如何?

B : It's nice.
很好。

A : It's not too bright?
會不會太鮮艷了?

B : No, it's fine. It goes well with that dress.
不會,很好。它和你的洋裝很配。

Dialogue 3

A : Your tan looks great!
　　你褐色的皮膚看起來很棒!

B : I just came back from Hawaii.
　　我剛從夏威夷回來。

A : Really? How long were you there?
　　真的啊?你去了多久?

B : Two weeks.
　　兩星期。

A : You look healthy.
　　你看起來很健康。

B : Thank you. I feel good.
　　謝謝你。我感覺很好。

〔舉一反三〕

A : That dress looks great on you.
　　那件洋裝穿在妳身上很好看。

B : Thank you.
　　謝謝你。

A : That blouse goes well with your skirt.
　　那件短上衣和妳的裙子很配。

B : Thank you. I had a difficult time finding one to
　　match.
　　謝謝你。我好不容易才配起來的。

A : Your drapes go well with your furniture. When did
　　you put them up?
　　你的窗帘和傢俱很配。你什麼時候掛上去的?

B : Just a few months ago.
　　幾個月前才掛的。

A : Where did you find these shoes? They match my purse perfectly.

你在哪裡買的鞋子？它們和我的皮包配極了。

B : I bought them at Carson's.

我在卡森店買的。

A : Sir, you need a tie to go with this suit.

先生，你需要一條領帶來配這套衣服。

B : I have several at home that'll match.

我家裡有幾條可以配的。

《背景說明》

　　每個人都喜歡受到稱讚，以下是幾種最容易使用的稱讚，請您牢記並善加運用。

　　「你穿（戴）～很好看。」*Your ~ looks good on you. That ~ looks great on you. You look handsome (or pretty) in ~.*

　　此外，形容兩件東西在一起很相配，用 A *goes well with* B.

【註釋】

go with 與～配合
tan〔tæn〕*n.* （皮膚經日曬而成的）褐色
Hawaii〔hə'waɪ·i〕*n.* 夏威夷
blouse〔blaʊz〕*n.* 短上衣
drape〔drep〕*n.* 窗帘
have a difficult time (*in*) ~*ing* 好不容易

55. May I ask you a question point-blank?

Dialogue 1

A : May I ask you a question point-blank?
我可不可以坦白地問你一個問題？

B : Sure, what is it?
當然，什麼問題？

A : Why are you quitting your job?
你為什麼辭職不幹了？

B : Would you like an honest answer?
你要一個誠實的回答嗎？

A : Of course.
當然。

B : This is a lousy company to work for.
這個公司很差勁。

Dialogue 2

A : I wonder what's wrong with Mary.
我想知道瑪莉怎麼了。

B : I've been wanting to ask her, but I don't know how.
我一直想問她，可是我不知道怎麼問。

A : Put it to her point-blank.
坦白地問她。

B : I don't think I can.
我想我沒辦法。

A : You have to. Maybe we can help her.
　　你得這麼做。或許我們能幫助她。

B : I'll speak to her this afternoon.
　　我今天下午會和她談。

Dialogue 3

A : I'd like to interview you for our high school
　　newspaper.
　　我想為我們中學的報紙訪問你。

B : Sure. Go right ahead.
　　當然。就開始吧。

A : Do you mind if I ask you some point-blank questions?
　　你介不介意我問你一些率直的問題？

B : Not at all.
　　一點也不。

A : O.K. When were you born?
　　好的。你什麼時候出生的？

B : I was born in 1943.
　　我一九四三年出生。

〔舉一反三〕

A : She told him point-blank not to call her anymore.
　　她坦白告訴他，以後不要再打電話給她。

B : Did he listen?
　　他聽了嗎？

A : I told him point-blank to take his feet off the
　　coffee table.
　　我率直地告訴他，把腳從咖啡桌拿開。

B : Good for you!
　　你真行！

A : Are you ready for some point-blank questions?
　　你準備好回答一些率直的問題嗎？
B : Fire away.
　　開始提問題吧。

A : If you ask point-blank whether she loves you, maybe she'll tell you.
　　如果你坦白問她愛不愛你，或許她會告訴你。
B : I hope so.
　　我希望如此。

A : Sometimes, it's wise to be direct with people.
　　有時候，對人直截了當是明智的。
B : You're right. Sometimes being frank is the best policy.
　　你說得對。有時候坦白是上策。

【註釋】

point-blank〔'pɔɪnt'blæŋk〕*adj.,adv.* 坦白的（地）；率直的（地）

quit〔kwɪt〕*vt.* 辭職；停止

lousy〔'lauzɪ〕*adj.*〔俚〕差勁的

go ahead 不猶豫地前進；做下去

fire away 繼續講下去，或提出問題

being frank is the best policy 坦白為上策，出自諺語：Honesty is the best policy. 誠實為上策。

56. The kitchen sink is clogged up.

Dialogue 1

A : Hello. This is Mr. Lee in apartment 203. My kitchen sink is clogged up.

哈囉。這是 203 公寓李先生。我家廚房的水槽阻塞了。

B : I'll send someone over as soon as possible.

我會儘快派人去。

A : I'd appreciate it. It's a real bother.

謝謝。這真的很困擾。

B : I understand.

我了解的。

A : By the way, when was the last time the exterminator was here?

順便一提，滅蟑螂、老鼠的人上次是什麼時候來的？

B : Last month. Do you have a problem in your apartment?

上個月。你的公寓有問題嗎？

Dialogue 2

A : Janitor.

管理員。

B : This is Mr. Yi in 356. My water faucet in the bathroom is dripping.

我是 356 的易先生。我浴室裡的水龍頭漏水。

A : I'll be up in a few minutes. Which apartment did you say you were in?

我過幾分鐘就來。你說你是哪一間的？

B : Apartment 356.

356 公寓。

A : O.K. I'll be right up.
　　好的。我馬上來。

B : Thank you. I'll be here.
　　謝謝你。我會在這裡。

Dialogue 3

A : Manager.
　　經理。

B : This is Bill Smith in apartment 1012-N. We don't have any hot water.
　　我是北棟 1012 號的比爾・史密斯。我們沒有熱水。

A : Did you contact the janitor?
　　你和管理員聯絡了嗎？

B : I tried to reach him, but there's no answer.
　　我試著聯絡他，但是沒有人接。

A : I'll send someone over immediately.
　　我會立刻派人去。

B : I'd appreciate it.
　　謝謝。

〔舉一反三〕

A : What's wrong with the drain?
　　排水管有什麼毛病？

B : It's clogged with hair.
　　被頭髮塞住了。

A : The toilet is clogged with tissue.
　　馬桶給衛生紙塞住了。

B : Don't use so much paper next time.
　　下次不要用太多衛生紙。

A : My toilet won't flush properly.
　　我的廁所沖水不好。

B : Get a plumber.
　　找個水管工人。

A : The drain is clogged and the water won't go down.
What should I do?
　　排水管阻塞了，水流不下去。我該怎麼辦？

B : Call the janitor.
　　打電話給管理員。

A : I'm hot. The air conditioner is out of order.
　　我很熱。冷氣機故障了。

B : Don't worry. It'll work in the winter.
　　別急。它冬天會正常操作的。

【註釋】

sink〔sɪŋk〕*n.* 水槽　　clog〔klɑg〕*vi.* 阻塞
bother〔'bɑðɚ〕*n.* 困擾；麻煩
exterminator〔ɪk'stɝmə,netɚ〕*n.* 以撲滅老鼠、蟑螂為業的人
janitor〔'dʒænətɚ〕*n.* 管理員；守衛
faucet〔'fɔsɪt〕*n.* 水龍頭
manager〔'mænɪdʒɚ〕*n.* 經理
drain〔dren〕*n.* 排水管　　tissue〔'tɪʃu〕*n.* 衛生紙
flush〔flʌʃ〕*vi.* (水)湧出　　plumber〔'plʌmɚ〕*n.* 水管工人
out of order 故障；壞了

57. He's tied up.

Dialogue 1

A : Good morning. Mr. Brown's office.
早安。布朗先生辦公室。

B : May I speak to Mr. Brown, please?
請找布朗先生聽電話好嗎？

A : I'm sorry, but he's tied up at the moment.
抱歉，他現在走不開。

B : When will he be free?
他什麼時候會有空？

A : I couldn't say. May I take a message?
我沒辦法說。要不要我給你留個話？

B : Yes, please have him call Mr. Chin as soon as possible.
好的，請他要儘快打電話給金先生。

Dialogue 2

A : Hi, Jane. Can you come over for lunch?
嗨，珍。妳能來吃中飯嗎？

B : I'm tied up with something urgent right now.
我現在忙著做一件緊急的事。

A : When will you be free?
你什麼時候有空？

B : Around 12:45. 十二點四十五分左右。

A : If you can make it, I'll wait for you.
如果你能來，我會等佗。

B : Fine. If this ties me up too long, I'll call you.
好的。如果這件事讓我辦太久，我會打電話給你。

Dialogue 3

A : Honey, can you tie this tie for me?

親愛的，你能幫我打這條領帶嗎？

B : Sure, I'll be there in a second.

當然，我馬上來。

A : I can't seem to get it tied properly this morning.

我今天早上似乎就是打不好。

B : I think you need new glasses.

我想你需要新眼鏡。

A : I don't think it's my vision. I'm just so tired lately.

我想不是我視力的問題。我只是最近很累。

B : Maybe you should call the doctor and have a physical exam.

或許你該打電話給醫生，去檢查身體。

〔舉一反三〕

A : May I speak to your mother?

請你媽媽聽電話好嗎？

B : She's tied up now. She's changing my brother's diaper.

她現在走不開。她正在給我弟弟換尿布。

A : Is Mr. Brown at his desk?

布朗先生在位子上嗎？

B : Yes, but he's tied up at the moment.

是的。但是他現在走不開。

A : Did you tie your own tie? It looks a little crooked.

你的領帶是自己打的嗎？看起來有點歪。

B : I'm glad you told me. I didn't notice it.

謝謝你告訴我。我沒注意到。

A : I'll be tied up with meetings all day.
　　我今天整天都要忙著開會。

B : Will you be free tomorrow?
　　你明天有空嗎?

A : Did you hear about the couple who were tied up
　　and robbed?
　　你聽說了那對夫婦被綁起來,而且被搶的事嗎?

B : No. Where did it happen?
　　沒有。在哪裡發生的?

《 背景説明 》

　　形容一個人很忙,有事情走不開,就説:*He is tied up.* 這句話比
He is busy. 更強調忙的情形。

　　例如有人問你:Can I see you for a moment? 回答:*I'm tied*
up with something urgent. 比説 I'm busy right now. 來得貼切。

　　又 tie 用在比賽中表示雙方同分。例如:Oxford *tied* Cambridge
in football. (牛津與劍橋的足球賽雙方打成平手。)或者説 The two
teams *tied.*

【註釋】

be tied up 忙碌;被綁緊
as ~ as possible = *as ~ as one can* 儘量~
urgent (ˈɝdʒənt) *adj.* 緊急的　　*make it* 順利;成功
vision (ˈvɪʒən) *n.* 視力　　*physical exam* 身體檢查
diaper (ˈdaɪəpɚ) *n.* 尿布
crooked (ˈkrukɪd) *adj.* 彎的;扭曲的

58. *Does it ring a bell?*

Dialogue 1

A : Hello. My name is Bob Jones. I really enjoyed your talk show.

哈囉。我叫鮑伯‧瓊斯。我眞的很喜歡你的訪問節目。

B : Thank you. I'm glad you did.

謝謝你。我很高興你喜歡它。

A : I'm trying to locate a friend of mine. Her name is Jane Shen.

我想找一個朋友。她叫沈珍。

B : I'm sorry, but the name doesn't ring a bell. Are you sure she's in Chicago?

抱歉，這個名字不熟。你確定她在芝加哥嗎？

A : I believe so. She was working here last year.

我相信如此。她去年在這裡工作。

B : Leave your number, and I'll see what I can do for you.

留下你的電話號碼，我會看看能爲你做什麼。

Dialogue 2

A : Did you ever hear about the restaurant on the lake front?

你聽說過湖濱的那家餐廳嗎？

B : No. I don't believe so.

沒有，我想沒有。

A : They're famous for their lobster.

他們以龍蝦聞名。

B : Lobster, yes, that rings a bell.

是的，龍蝦，似乎很熟。

Dialogue 3

A : Guess who I met at the grocery store.
猜猜看我在雜貨店遇到誰了。

B : I can't imagine.
我猜不出來。

A : Do you remember Mr. Johnson from our old neighborhood?
你記得過去住在我們附近的強生先生嗎？

B : That name rings a bell, but I can't place him.
那個名字很熟，但是我說不出他住哪裡。

A : He used to live in the building next to ours.
他過去住在我們隔壁一棟樓。

B : Oh yes, now I remember. He had dark hair and wore glasses.
哦，我現在想起來了。他頭髮黑的，而且戴眼鏡。

〔舉一反三〕

A : Mr. Bob Smith from Taiwan University called while you were out.
你出去的時候，台灣大學的鮑伯・史密斯打電話來。

B : That name doesn't ring a bell.
那個名字不熟。

A : Do you know that man?
你認識那個人嗎？

B : No. I don't remember ever meeting him.
不，我不記得曾經見過他。

A : Do you know Edward Kennedy?
你知道愛德華・甘迺迪嗎？

B : That name rings a bell. He's our senator!
那個名字很熟。他是我們的參議員！

A：Does the address seem familiar to you?

這個地址你熟嗎？

B：No, it doesn't ring a bell.

不，不熟。

A：Do you remember where his hometown is? I think it's somewhere in Wisconsin.

你記得他的家鄉在哪裡嗎？我想是在威斯康辛州的某個地方。

B：That rings a bell.

那很熟。

【註釋】

talk show 訪問節目

locate〔lo'ket〕*vt.* 找出

ring a bell 引起反應；使某人想起某事

lobster〔'labstɚ〕*n.* 龍蝦

Wisconsin〔wɪs'kɑnsn̩〕*n.* 威斯康辛州（美國中北部的一州）

59. I can't express myself very well in English.

Dialogue 1

A : How long have you been in the United States, Mr. Wang?

王先生，你在美國待多久了？

B : Oh, a little over five years.

哦，五年多一點。

A : Are you a U.S. citizen?

你是美國公民嗎？

B : Yes, I am.

是的，我是。

A : Your English must be very good.

你的英文一定很好。

B : It's O.K., but sometimes I can't express myself very well in English.

還可以。但是有時候我沒有辦法用英文表達得很好。

Dialogue 2

A : Would you accompany me on my interview with the IBM Company?

你願意陪我去 IBM 公司面談嗎？

B : Why can't you go alone?

你為什麼不能一個人去呢？

A : I can't express myself very well in English.

我沒辦法用英文表達得很好。

B : I understand. You need a little moral support.

我明白了。你需要一點精神支援。

A : I guess that's what it is.
　　我想是的。

B : Sure. I'll be happy to go with you.
　　好的。我樂意和你一起去。

Dialogue 3

A : I'd like to spend some time with you.
　　我想和你在一起。

B : Why? 為什麼？

A : I like you.
　　我喜歡你。

B : I don't understand exactly what you are trying to say.
　　我不很了解你想說什麼。

A : I can't express it very well in English, but I believe you call it a date.
　　我沒辦法用英文表達得很好，但我相信你稱它為約會。

B : Oh, I see. You're asking me out!
　　好的，我明白了。你在邀我出去！

〔舉一反三〕

A : Do you think you can speak at the next meeting?
　　你認為你下次會議能發言嗎？

B : I'll try, but it's very difficult for me to express myself in English.
　　我會試試看，但是要我用英文表達自己很困難。

A : How do you prefer your beef?
　　你的牛肉要怎樣的？

B : I'm not sure of the English expression, but don't overcook it.
　　我不大確定英文怎麼說，但不要煮太久。

A : What type of girls do you prefer?
   你喜歡哪種類型的女孩？
B : That's very difficult for me to express in English.
   我很難用英文表達。

A : What are you trying to explain?
   你想要解釋什麼？
B : It's very difficult for me to explain my ideas in English.
   我很難用英文表達想法。

A : I'd like to explain how I feel about you, but it is very difficult for me to express my feelings in English.
   我想說明我對你的感覺，但是我很難用英文表達我的感情。
B : You don't have to say anything. I understand.
   你什麼也不必說。我了解。

【註釋】

moral（'mɔrəl）*adj.* 精神上的

ask sb. out 邀～出去

feelings（'filɪŋz）*n. pl.* 感情（常用複數）

60. *Are you going to the States for good?*

Dialogue 1

A : We plan to go to the United States.
我們計劃要去美國。

B : Oh! When are you going?
哦！你們什麼時候走？

A : September 19th.
九月十九號。

B : Are you going to the States for good?
你們要去美國永久定居嗎？

A : Yes, we are.
是的，我們要永久定居。

B : I hope you enjoy it there.
我希望你們在那裡愉快。

Dialogue 2

A : Mr. Yi, I want to say goodbye to you and your family.
易先生，我想和你及你的家人說再見。

B : Why, Mr. Carson? Where are you going?
為什麼，卡森先生？你要去哪裡？

A : I'm going to Germany to visit my brother.
我要去德國看我的弟弟。

B : Are you going there for good?
你要永遠留在那裡嗎？

A : No. It's just for a visit.
不，只是去探望一下。

B : I hope you have a good trip.
我希望你旅途愉快。

Dialogue 3

A : Mr. Johnson, would you be interested in an opening we have in Los Angeles?
強生先生，你對我們洛杉磯的空缺有興趣嗎？

B : I really don't know. Could you tell me more about it?
我眞的不知道。你能多告訴我一些關於它的事嗎？

A : Certainly. You would be the general manager of the West Coast office.
當然。你將成爲西海岸辦公室的總經理。

B : It sounds good. Would we have to stay in Los Angeles for good?
似乎不錯。我們得永遠留在洛杉磯嗎？

A : I can't answer that at this time.
現在我沒辦法回答那個問題。

B : May I have a day or two to think it over?
我可不可以考慮一兩天？

〔舉一反三〕

A : Are you leaving the city for good?
你要永遠離開這個城市嗎？

B : Yes. I have to live in a warmer climate.
是的，我必須住在比較暖和的氣候區。

A : Do you think your dog is gone for good?
　　你想你的狗永遠不見了嗎?

B : I don't know.
　　我不知道。

A : Are you going to Japan for good?
　　你要永遠留在日本嗎?

B : I think so.
　　我想是的。

A : Do you think he will leave for good?
　　你認為他會永遠離開嗎?

B : I think he will.
　　我想他會。

A : May I keep this book?
　　我能留著這本書嗎?

B : Yes, you may.
　　是的,你可以。

【註釋】

for good 永久地　　opening〔'opənɪŋ〕*n.* 空缺
general manager 總經理　　*think over* 考慮

61. *For the time being*.

Dialogue 1

A : What did you do before you came to this country?
你在還沒來這個國家之前從事什麼工作?

B : I was an accountant.
我是個會計師。

A : What do you do now?
你現在做什麼呢?

B : For the time being I'm working at a bank as a janitor.
目前暫時在一家銀行做清潔工。

A : I'm sure you'll be very successful in the future.
我相信你將來一定會非常成功。

B : Thank you. I hope so. Once I learn the language.
謝謝你,我希望如此。只要我學會這種語言。

Dialogue 2

A : Why are you riding the bus?
你為什麼搭公車?

B : My car's in the garage again.
我的車子又進修理廠了。

A : I thought you were going to buy a new car.
我以為你要買一部新車。

B : I was, but I can't afford one right now.
我是要買,但是目前我還付不起。

A : What are you going to do for transportation?
你的交通問題如何解決?

B : For the time being I'll have to ride the bus.
目前我必須搭公車。

Dialogue 3

A : Has Jack found a job yet?
　　傑克找到工作了嗎？

B : No. He's still looking.
　　沒有，他仍然在找。

A : He's been out of work for a long time.
　　他失業已經好久了。

B : Yes. He's getting discouraged.
　　是啊，他開始感到氣餒了。

A : Where's he living now?
　　他現在住在哪裏？

B : For the time being he's staying with his parents.
　　暫時和他的父母同住。

〔舉一反三〕

A : Did your sister find an apartment yet?
　　你妹妹找到公寓了嗎？

B : No. She's staying with me for the time being.
　　沒有。她暫時和我同住。

A : How is your leg?
　　你的腿怎樣？

B : Better, but for the time being I have to use a cane.
　　好多了，但目前我必須用拐杖。

A : Did Jane see me?
　　珍看到我了嗎？

B : No. You're safe for the time being.
　　沒有，你暫時很安全。

A : Could you lend me some money?

　　你能借我一些錢嗎？

B : Sorry. For the time being I'm broke.

　　抱歉，我現在沒錢。

A : I thought your son was going to get married.

　　我以為你兒子要結婚了。

B : He'll get married next year. For the time being he's still a bachelor.

　　他將在明年結婚。目前他仍然是個單身漢。

【註釋】

What do you do? 你從事什麼職業？

accountant〔əˋkauntənt〕*n.* 會計師

for the time being 暫時

janitor〔ˋdʒænətɚ〕*n.* 清潔工；工友；管理員

garage〔gəˋrɑdʒ〕*n.* 車庫；修車廠

broke〔brok〕*adj.* 一文不名；沒錢

cane〔ken〕*n.* 手杖

transportation〔͵trænspɚˋteʃən〕*n.* 運輸工具；交通

be out of work 失業

bachelor〔ˋbætʃəlɚ〕*n.* 單身漢

62. *I'm calling about the apartment you advertised.*

Dialogue 1

A : Hello. I'm calling about the apartment you advertised.

哈囉！我打電話是想問一下有關你登廣告的公寓。

B : Yes. Can I help you?

是的，我能幫你什麼忙嗎？

A : I'm interested in a two-bedroom apartment. Is it available?

我喜歡有兩間臥房的公寓。有空的嗎？

B : Yes, it is.

是的，有空的。

A : What's the rent?

租金多少呢？

B : It's $400 a month.

一個月四百塊。

Dialogue 2

A : Is this apartment furnished or unfurnished?

這公寓有沒有附傢俱？

B : It's unfurnished.

沒附傢俱的。

A : How many bedrooms does it have?

有多少間臥室？

B : Three bedrooms.

三間臥室。

A : Who pays the utilities?
　　誰付水電雜費呢？
B : You have to pay.
　　你必須付。

Dialogue 3

A : I'm calling about the room you advertised. Is it still available?
　　我打電話是想知道有關你刊登廣告的房間。它仍然空著嗎？
B : Yes, it is. What would you like to know about it?
　　是的，它仍然空著。你想知道些什麼？

A : Does it have a private entrance?
　　它有沒有私人進出口？
B : Yes, it does. You also have kitchen privileges with the room.
　　是的，它有。租這間房間你也有使用廚房的權利。

A : Is there a place to park my car?
　　有沒有地方讓我停車？
B : Yes. Why don't you come by and look at the room?
　　有的。你何不過來看看房子？

〔舉一反三〕

A : I'm calling about the apartment you advertised.
　　我打電話是想問一下有關你登廣告的公寓。
B : I'm sorry. I've already rented it.
　　很抱歉，我已經將它租出去了。

A : Is there a garage with the apartment?
　　這公寓有沒有車庫？
B : No, but there is a parking space.
　　沒有，但是有停車位置。

A : Does the bathroom have a shower?
　　浴室有沒有淋浴？

B : Yes, it does. It's all new.
　　有的，它是全新的。

A : Is the heat gas or electric?
　　暖氣是用瓦斯還是用電？

B : The heat is gas, the stove is electric.
　　暖氣用瓦斯，爐子用電。

A : Who pays the utilities?
　　誰付水電等雜費？

B : You have to take care of them.
　　你必須自己負責。

【註釋】

advertise〔͵ædvɚˋtaɪz, ˋædvɚ͵taɪz〕*vt.* 登廣告

Is it available？有空的嗎？有適合的嗎？

furnish〔ˋfɝnɪʃ〕*vt.* 陳設；佈置（通常租屋帶有傢俱或不帶傢俱，用 furnished 或 unfurnished 來形容，不用 furnitured 或 unfurnitured。）

utility〔juˋtɪlətɪ〕*n.* 有益；效用（utilities 通常指水費、電費等雜費。）

private entrance 私人用的出入口

privilege〔ˋprɪvḷɪdʒ〕*n.* 特權；特殊利益

kitchen privilege 使用廚房的權利

come by 順路造訪　　　shower〔ˋʃauɚ〕*n.* 淋浴

heat〔hit〕*n.* 屋中之暖氣　　*take care of* 處理；負～之責

63. I'd like to have telephone service.

Dialogue 1

A : Operator 307. May I help you?
   307 號接線生。我能幫你忙嗎？

B : Yes, I'd like to have telephone service.
   是的，我想要裝電話。

A : Do you presently have service?
   你目前裝有電話嗎？

B : No. This is new service.
   沒有，這是新申請。

A : All right. I'll connect you with our main business office.
   好的，我把你接到我們的業務總部。

B : Thank you.
   謝謝你。

Dialogue 2

A : Janet Smith. May I help you?
   珍尼特·史密絲，我能幫你忙嗎？

B : Yes, I'd like to have some information about having a phone installed.
   是的，我想知道些有關裝電話的資料。

A : At what address?
   地址是什麼？

B : 3725 W. Lawrence.
   西勞倫斯 3725 號。

A : Have you had service before?
　　你以前曾裝過電話嗎？

B : No, we're new to the city.
　　沒有，我們是新來到這城市。

Dialogue 3

A : We'd like a red, table model, touch phone.
　　我們想要一個紅色桌上型的按鍵電話。

B : All right. When do you want service installed?
　　好的。你什麼時候要安裝呢？

A : Next Thursday, if possible.
　　下星期四，如果可能的話。

B : What's your name and address?
　　你的姓名、地址是什麼？

A : 4526 N. Broadway. The name is Chen, C-H-E-N.
　　北百老匯 4526 號。姓陳，耳東陳。

B : The installer will be there sometime between 8 a.m. and 6 p.m.
　　電話裝設人員將在早上八點到下午六點之間到你那兒。

〔舉一反三〕

A : Illinois Bell. May I help you?
　　這裏是伊利諾貝爾電話公司。我能幫你什麼忙嗎？

B : Yes. I'd like to have telephone service.
　　是的。我想要裝電話。

A : Business office, Jane Smith. May I help you?
　　業務部，珍·史密絲。我能幫你什麼忙嗎？

B : Yes, I'd like to have some information about having a phone installed.
　　是的，我想要一些有關裝設電話的資料。

A : We've just moved into the city. I'd like to have a phone installed.

我們剛剛搬來這城市。我想裝個電話。

B : May I have your name and address?

我能知道你的姓名和地址嗎？

A : What would be the earliest date for installation?

最快哪一天能安裝？

B : I can schedule you for next Tuesday.

我可以幫你訂在下星期二。

A : I'd like to have my telephone disconnected.

我想把電話停掉。

B : What day would you like your service to end?

你希望哪一天停掉電話呢？

【註釋】

Operator 307. = **This is operator 307 speaking.**
Janet Smith. = **This is Janet Smith speaking.** 電話接通後先自報
姓名等。通常省去 "This is … speaking."。

telephone service 電話服務，指裝電話。

install〔ɪn'stɔl〕vt. 裝設；安置

business office 業務部門

touch phone 按鍵、觸鍵式電話

schedule〔'skɛdʒul〕vt. 安排（某事）於將來某特定的日期；排定

disconnect〔,dɪskə'nɛkt〕vt. 不接通，指「停掉電話」而言。

64. How do you like America?

Dialogue 1

A : How do you like America?
　　你喜歡美國嗎？

B : I like it here very much.
　　我非常喜歡這裏。

A : What do you like most?
　　你最喜歡哪一點？

B : I like the vastness and the beautiful scenery.
　　我喜歡遼闊無垠的幅員和美麗的風景。

A : What was one of your first impressions of this country?
　　你對這個國家的第一個印象是什麼？

B : The orderly fashion in which the American people conduct themselves.
　　美國人舉止上井然有序的作風。

Dialogue 2

A : How do you like Taiwan?
　　你喜歡台灣嗎？

B : So far, I'm enjoying it.
　　到目前為止，我還蠻喜歡它的。

A : Is this your first time to visit the island?
　　這是你第一次來拜訪這個島嗎？

B : Yes, it is.
　　是的。

A : Have you had the opportunity to travel around here?

你有機會四處旅行嗎？

B : Yes. We've been to Mt. Jade and found it absolutely breath-taking.

有的，我們曾經去過玉山，發現那裡眞是令人心驚肉跳。

Dialogue 3

A : How long have you been in Taiwan?

你來台灣多久了？

B : Almost two years now.

到現在快兩年了。

A : How do you like Taipei?

你喜歡台北嗎？

B : I think it's very exciting. There's so much to do and see.

我認爲很刺激。有很多可做及可看的。

A : How much longer do you plan to stay?

你計劃再停留多久？

B : I think I'll be going back home in the middle of next year.

我想我明年年中回去。

〔舉一反三〕

A : How do you like America?

你喜歡美國嗎？

B : I like it very much.

我很喜歡。

A : How do you like living here?
　　你喜歡住在這裡嗎?

B : Fine, but it's so different from my own country.
　　喜歡，但是這裡和我自己的國家大不相同。

A : What is your first impression of our country?
　　你對我們國家的第一印象是什麼?

B : There's so much to do and see.
　　有非常多可做和可看的。

A : What do you think of our people?
　　你認爲我們的人民怎樣?

B : They are so friendly and willing to help each other.
　　他們很友善，而且樂意互相幫助。

A : Are you enjoying your stay in our country?
　　你在我們國家過得愉快嗎?

B : Yes, very much.
　　是的，非常愉快。

【註釋】

vastness (ˈvæstnɪs) n. 遼闊

scenery (ˈsinərɪ) n. 風景

orderly (ˈɔrdəlɪ) adj. 有秩序的

conduct oneself 舉止

so far 到目前爲止

breath-taking (ˈbrɛθˌtekɪŋ) adj. 令人心驚肉跳的;使人興奮的

65. *God bless you!*

Dialogue 1

A : (*a sneeze*) Excuse me.
（打噴嚏）對不起。

B : God bless you!
願老天保佑你！

A : Thank you. 謝謝。

B : It sounds like you're coming down with a cold.
你好像著涼了。

A : I'm afraid so.
我想恐怕是的。

B : You'd better take care. There're a lot of colds going around.
你最好保重點。現在感冒正在流行。

Dialogue 2

A : (*a sneeze*) Excuse me.
（打噴嚏）對不起。

B : God bless you!
願上帝保佑你！

A : Thanks. 謝了。

B : You've been sneezing a lot lately, are you all right?
你最近經常打噴嚏，你還好吧？

A : Oh, I've got a terrible cold.
噢，我得了重感冒。

B : I'm sorry to hear that.
我很難過聽到這事。

Dialogue 3

A : (*a sneeze*) Pardon me.
　　(打噴嚏)眞抱歉。

B : Gesundheit!
　　祝你健康!

A : Thank you.
　　謝謝。

B : Are you coming down with something?
　　你該不會得了什麼病吧?

A : No, I have allergies this time of the year.
　　不是的,我每年這個時候都會過敏。

B : Well, do take care.
　　喔,得多保重。

〔舉一反三〕

A : Excuse me.
　　對不起。

B : God bless you!
　　上帝保佑你!

A : God bless you!
　　上帝保佑你!

B : Thank you.
　　謝謝。

A : Pardon me.
　　原諒我。

B : Gesundheit!
　　祝你健康!

A : May God bless you and your family.
　　願上帝保佑你和你的家人。

B : And you and yours, too.
　　以及你和你的家人。

A : May God speed you on your trip.
　　願上帝祝福你旅途事事順遂。

B : Thank you.
　　謝謝。

《背景説明》

　　God bless you! 可以表示「願上帝保佑你！多可憐啊！」最常用在別人打噴嚏之後。自己打了噴嚏，應立刻說：*Excuse me.* 或 *Pardon me.* 表示歉意。對方則會說 *God bless you*! 或 *Bless you*!

【註釋】

sneeze〔sniz〕*n.* 噴嚏　*vi.* 打噴嚏

God bless you. 上帝保佑你。（美國人在別人打噴嚏時，常說這句話。）

come down with 罹患～

There are a lot of colds going around. 感冒正在流行。

lately〔'letlɪ〕*adv.* 最近；近來

gesundheit〔gə'zunthaɪt〕*interj.*〔德〕乾杯時，或向剛打噴嚏的人祝健康之感歎詞。

allergy〔'ælɚdʒɪ〕*n.* 過敏症；過敏性反應

God speed you. 上帝祝福你。

　　May God speed you on your trip. 願上帝祝福你旅途順心。

66. *How large is your party?*

Dialogue 1

A : Good evening, sir. May I help you?
先生，晚安。有我可效勞的地方嗎？

B : Yes. What kind of rooms do you have?
是的。你們有些什麼樣的房間？

A : How large is your party?
你們一群有多少人？

B : Three. Two adults and one child.
三個。兩個大人和一個小孩。

A : Let's see. We have a room with two double beds. How many nights?
讓我瞧瞧。我們有一個有兩張雙人床的房間。要住幾晚？

B : Only overnight. 只過一晚。

Dialogue 2

A : May I help you, sir?
我可以效勞嗎，先生？

B : I'd like to reserve a table for dinner.
我想預訂一張晚餐的桌位。

A : Certainly, sir. How large is your party?
當然可以。你們一群有多少人？

B : Six couples. 六對夫婦。

A : Would you like to reserve a private dining room?
你要保留一間個別的餐室嗎？

B : That sounds like a good idea.
似乎是個好主意。

Dialogue 3

A : I'd like to reserve some seats for the opera.
　　我想預訂一些歌劇的座位。

B : How many are in your group, sir?
　　你們一群有多少人，先生？

A : Ten.
　　十位。

B : I have ten seats together in the orchestra section.
　　我在靠近舞台的首席區有十個相連的座位。

A : Good. I'll take those.
　　很好，我就要這些。

B : Here you are. That'll be $ 70.00.
　　這些給你。一共是七十元。

〔舉一反三〕

A : I'd like to reserve a table for dinner.
　　我想預訂一張晚餐桌位。

B : How large is your party, sir?
　　你們一群有多少人，先生？

A : How many are in your group, sir?
　　你們有多少人，先生？

B : We'll need six tickets.
　　我們需要六張票。

A : Are you going to need any extra chairs?
　　你們會不會需要一些額外的椅子？

B : Yes. We're expecting a large party.
　　是的。我們預期有一大群人。

A：We'll have some extra people over for dinner.
　　我們有額外增加的人過來用晚餐。

B：How large a group are you expecting?
　　你想會有多少人?

A：How many people will be here tonight?
　　今晚會有多少人來?

B：About ten.
　　大概十個。

《 背景説明 》

　　當你到旅館的櫃台詢問有沒有房間時，對方會問你：*How large is your party*?如果你回答：We're not going to have a party. We want to sleep here. 是會鬧笑話的。

　　party 在此是指「團體；群」，不指「宴會」，*a party of five* 是有五個成員的一群人。因此，再遇到買票、訂座位、訂房間時，對 *How large is your party*?的回答，直接説人數(如：*Five*.或*Ten*.)即可。

【註釋】

How large is your party?＝How many are in your group?
　　都是詢問對方一群一共有多少人的問法。
adult〔ə'dʌlt,'ædʌlt〕n. 成人　adj. 成人的
double bed 雙人床　***single bed*** 單人床
overnight〔'ovə'naɪt〕adv. 過夜地
reserve〔rɪ'zɜv〕vt. 保留；預訂
opera〔'ɑpərə〕n. 歌劇
orchestra section 通常指靠近管弦樂團 (舞台) 位置的首席座位。
extra〔'ɛkstrə〕adj. 額外的

67. *Could you speak up, please?*

Dialogue 1

A : This report must be ready by Monday.
這份報告星期一以前必須做好。

B : Excuse me sir, could you speak up, please? I'm having trouble hearing you in the back of the room.
真抱歉，先生，能不能請你說大聲一點？我在房間後面聽不見。

A : Yes, of course.
好的，當然可以。

B : Now what did you say about the report?
那麼你剛才說那報告怎樣？

A : I said, it must be ready by Monday.
我說，在星期一以前要準備好。

B : I understand. 我知道了。

Dialogue 2

A : Can you people in the back hear me?
你們在後面的人能聽到我說話嗎？

B : No, we can't.
不行，我們聽不到。

A : I'm sorry. I'll try to speak up.
真抱歉。我會試著說大聲點。

B : We still can't hear you.
我們仍然聽不到你。

A : (*speaking louder*) Is this better?
（說得更大聲點）這樣好些了嗎？

B : Yes. That's fine. 是的。好多了。

Dialogue 3

A : I can hardly hear you.
　　我幾乎不能聽到你的聲音。

B : We seem to have a bad connection on this phone.
　　我們的電話線好像接得不大好。

A : Could you speak up?
　　你能不能說大聲點？

B : I'm talking as loud as I can.
　　我已經盡可能地大聲了。

A : I'm going to hang up and call you back.
　　我要把電話掛掉，然後再打給你。

B : Good idea.
　　好主意。

〔舉一反三〕

A : Could you speak up, please?
　　請你說大聲些好嗎？

B : Of course. I'm sorry.
　　當然可以。對不起。

A : Do you have a question?
　　你們有問題嗎？

B : No, but could you speak up? We can't hear you.
　　沒有，但是能不能請你說大聲點？我們聽不到你。

A : Can you hear him?
　　你能聽到他嗎？

B : No, I wish he'd speak up.
　　不能，我希望他能說大聲點。

A : He speaks very softly, doesn't he?
　　他說話非常輕，不是嗎？

B : Yes, I wish he'd speak louder.
　　是的，我希望他說話能大聲些。

A : Let's sit in the front so we can hear.
　　我們坐在前面好聽得到。

B : Right. He speaks very softly.
　　沒錯。他說話聲音太輕了。

《背景説明》

　　在開會或對話中，有時會碰到對方說話的聲音太小，無法聽清楚；此時可以要求對方說大聲一點，用：*Could you speak up, please?* 或 *Could you speak louder, please?*

　　如果是說得太快了，就要用 *Could you speak a little more slowly?*「請你說慢一點好嗎？」或者用 *I can't follow you.*「我聽不懂。」

【註釋】

speak up 大聲說　　*in the back* 在後面
connection (kə'nɛkʃən) *n.* 聯繫；連接
as loud as … can 儘可能的大聲　　*hang up* 掛斷電話
in the front 在前面

68. *I enjoyed your company*.

Dialogue 1

A : I really must be going now, it's getting late.
　　我現在一定要走，已經晚了。

B : Oh, can't you stay a little longer?
　　哦，你能不能再多待一會兒？

A : No. I really must be running.
　　不，我真的一定得趕快走。

B : Well, I enjoyed your company.
　　呃，我喜歡有你作伴。

A : Yes, we should get together more often.
　　是的，我們應該更常在一起的。

B : I think so, too. 我也這樣認為。

Dialogue 2

A : Sue, your party was lovely.
　　蘇，妳的宴會真令人愉快。

B : I'm so glad you enjoyed it.
　　我很高興你喜歡它。

A : Your home is charming. It's so comfortable.
　　妳的家很迷人，它真舒適。

B : Thank you for saying that.
　　謝謝你這麼說。

A : Everything was perfect. Thank you for inviting me.
　　一切都好極了。謝謝妳邀請我。

B : I enjoyed your company.
　　我很喜歡有你作伴。

Dialogue 3

A : Hi, Bill. What are you doing here?

嗨，比爾。你在這兒幹嘛？

B : Oh, I missed my train. I have to wait until three for the next one.

哦，我沒趕上火車。我必須等到三點才有下一班車。

A : That's too bad.

眞不幸。

B : Why are you here?

你爲什麼在這兒？

A : I'm supposed to meet a friend at two-thirty.

我兩點半要在這兒會一個朋友。

B : Why don't you keep me company while you wait?

當你等時，何不跟我作伴？

〔舉一反三〕

A : I had a lovely time this afternoon.

今天下午我過得很愉快。

B : Thank you. I enjoyed your company.

謝謝你。我喜歡和你作伴。

A : I enjoyed your company. Thanks for coming.

我喜歡有你爲伴，謝謝賞光。

B : I enjoyed being with you, too.

我也喜歡和你在一起。

A : Could you keep me company while I wait?

你能不能陪我等？

B : Sure. Let's go have some coffee.

當然可以。我們去喝點咖啡吧。

A：Tom's good company, isn't he?
　　湯姆是個好伴侶，不是嗎？

B：Yes, he is. He's a lot of fun.
　　是的，他是的。他很有趣。

A：We're having company for dinner.
　　我們有朋友要來晚餐。

B：Who's coming?
　　誰要來？

【註釋】

company (ˈkʌmpənɪ) n. 伴侶；一群人
charming (ˈtʃɑrmɪŋ) adj. 迷人的
be supposed to 應當
keep sb. **company** 陪伴某人

> I had a lovely time this afternoon.

> Thank you. I enjoyed your company.

69. We have three holidays in a row.

Dialogue 1

A : The new year will be here before you know it.
一不注意，新年又快到了！

B : This year really went by fast.
今年過得眞快。

A : It seems every year goes by faster.
好像一年比一年過得快。

B : I especially enjoy New Year's, though.
雖然如此，我仍然特別喜歡過新年。

A : Why? 爲什麼？

B : We have three holidays in a row.
我們有一連放三天的假期。

Dialogue 2

A : Okay, Tom, pay off our bet!
O.K. 湯姆，付賭金吧！

B : You mean my team lost again?
你的意思是說我那一隊又輸了？

A : They sure did. 他們當然輸了。

B : Wow! That's three games in a row.
喔！一連輸了三場。

A : They'll improve.
他們會改進的。

B : They'd better. Their losing streak is getting
expensive for me.
他們最好是如此。他們這陣敗勢對我來說是愈來愈花錢了。

Dialogue 3

A : This weather has been terrible.
　　最近天氣很糟糕。

B : I agree. It's been raining forever.
　　我同意，雨會永遠不停地下。

A : Not really! It just seems that way.
　　不真是如此！只是好像是那樣罷了。

B : It's been raining steadily for the past five days.
　　雨已經連綿不斷地下了五天了。

A : It's supposed to stop tomorrow.
　　它明天應該會停。

B : I hope so! Everything I own is wet!
　　我希望如此！我的每樣東西都是濕的。

〔舉一反三〕

A : We have three holidays in a row. Are you going anywhere?
　　我們有一連三天的假期，你要上哪兒去嗎？

B : Yes. I'm going to visit my hometown.
　　是的，我想回老家去探望探望。

A : My favorite team has won five games in a row.
　　我最喜愛的球隊已經連贏了五場。

B : Great! Maybe they'll be the new champions.
　　太好了！也許他們將成為新的冠軍隊。

A : Is Tom late again?
　　湯姆又遲到了嗎？

B : Yes. This is the third consecutive day.
　　是的。這是連續的第三天。

A : That boxer has scored five knockouts in a row.
　　那拳擊手已經連續五次擊倒對方而得分。

B : He's a tough fighter.
　　他是個強勁的打者。

A : Is his wife going to have another baby?
　　他太太又要生孩子了嗎?

B : Yes. They want a boy. They've had three girls in a row.
　　是的,他們要個男孩。他們已經連生了三個女孩了。

【註釋】

　~ before you know it 在知道前就~;還沒注意到就~
　row〔ro〕*n.* 行列;排;一連串　　*in a row* 接連
　pay off 付清　　streak〔strik〕*n.* 短時間;陣
　champion〔'tʃæmpɪən〕*n.* 冠軍;優勝者
　consecutive〔kən'sɛkjətɪv〕*adj.* 連續不斷的;接連而至的
　knockout〔'nɑk͵aut〕*n.* (拳擊)擊昏;打敗
　tough fighter 強壯有韌性的拳擊手

70. *Please make yourself at home.*

Dialogue 1

A : Please come in and make yourself at home.
　　請進，不要拘束。

B : Thank you. You have a beautiful house.
　　謝謝。你有個漂亮的房子。

A : Thank you. Let me take your coat.
　　謝謝，我來拿你的外套。

B : All right. 好的。

A : Won't you have a seat?
　　你不坐下嗎？

B : Yes, thank you.
　　好的，謝謝。

Dialogue 2

A : Good evening, won't you come in?
　　晚安，不進來坐坐？

B : Thank you. 謝謝。

A : Please make yourself comfortable.
　　請不要客氣。

B : I can only stay a few minutes.
　　我只能停留幾分鐘。

A : Do you have time for a cup of coffee before you
　　rush off?
　　在你急著離開前，有沒有時間喝杯咖啡？

B : Well, maybe a half cup, thanks.
　　嗯，也許半杯可以，謝謝你。

Dialogue 3

A : Good morning, please come in.
早安，請進。

B : Thanks.
謝了。

A : I'll be with you in a moment, I'm on the phone.
Please make yourself at home.
我在講電話，一會兒就來陪你。請不要拘束。

B : O.K.
好的。

A : (*after call*) Sorry about the interruption.
（打完電話）剛才被打斷，眞抱歉。

B : Oh, that's quite all right.
噢，沒關係。

〔舉一反三〕

A : May I sit here?
我能坐這兒嗎？

B : Sure. Make yourself at home.
當然可以。不要客氣。

A : Come in. Make yourself at home.
請進，不要客氣。

B : Thanks.
謝了。

A : Feel free to look around. Make yourself at home.
四處隨便看看，請不要客氣。

B : Thank you. You have a lovely apartment.
謝謝。你有個可愛的公寓。

A : Have a seat. Make yourself comfortable.
　　請坐。不要拘束。

B : May I leave my package here?
　　我能把行李留在這兒嗎？

A : Can I get you anything?
　　要不要我拿些東西給你？

B : No, thank you. I'm comfortable.
　　不了，謝謝你。我很舒服。

【註釋】

make *oneself* **at home** 不要拘束

have a seat 坐下

rush 〔rʌʃ〕 *vi.* 急促；匆忙

rush off 匆忙離去

on the phone 正在通電話中

interruption 〔,ɪntə'rʌpʃən〕 *n.* 打岔；中斷（談話、做事）

Sure. Make yourself at home.

May I sit here?

71. After you, please.

Dialogue 1

(*A opens the door for B*)
(A 替 B 開門)

A : After you, please.
　　你先走，請。

B : Thank you.
　　謝謝。

A : This is a beautiful car. What make is it?
　　這是輛漂亮的車子。它是什麼廠牌的？

B : It's an '83 Lincoln Continental.
　　它是 83 年的林肯大陸型。

A : Wow. You must be very rich.
　　喔，你一定非常有錢。

B : I wish it were mine, but it's my father's.
　　我希望它是我的，但是它是我爸爸的。

Dialogue 2

A : How long do you think we'll have to wait for a
　　table?
　　你認為我們要等多久才會有桌位？

B : It shouldn't be much longer.
　　應該不會太久。

A : Oh, look, there're some people leaving now.
　　喔，瞧，有人現在要走了。

B : That should be our table.
　　那應該是我們的桌位。

A：Oh, good. Let's go.
　　喔，眞好。咱們過去吧！

B：After you, please.
　　你先走，請。

Dialogue 3

A：How long have you been waiting in line?
　　你在這兒排隊等了多久？

B：I've been waiting for twenty minutes.
　　我已經等了二十分鐘。

A：Would you mind if I went ahead of you?
　　你介意我走在你前頭嗎？

B：Why?
　　爲什麼？

A：I'm on my lunch hour and I'm already late.
　　現在是我的午餐時間，而我早就遲了。

B：O.K. Go ahead of me.
　　好吧，走在我前面吧。

〔舉一反三〕

A：After you, please.
　　您先請。

B：Thank you.
　　謝了。

A：Would you like to go ahead of me?
　　你要不要走在我前頭？

B：If you don't mind. Thank you.
　　如果你不介意的話。謝謝你。

A : Let me hold the door for you.
　　我幫你扶住這門。

B : Thank you.
　　謝謝你。

A : I'll follow you.
　　我跟著你。

B : All right.
　　好的。

A : Go ahead of me, please.
　　走在我前頭，請。

B : Thank you.
　　謝了。

┌─《背景説明》────────────────

　　After you, please.「你先請。」是客氣的表示。在進入餐廳、排隊購物或上車時，表示禮讓對方，就說這句話。此時對方應回答：Thank you. 尤其是有女性同伴在場時，更應記住 Ladies first. 的原則，常說 *After you, please.* 並不吃虧。

└──────────────────────────

【註釋】

What make is it? 問車子或其他產品的年份、廠牌、型號等用 "make"。
continental〔͵kɑntə'nɛntḷ〕*adj.* 大陸的
Lincoln Continental 為美國福特公司出品之林肯牌豪華型轎車。
in line 排隊
go ahead of 走在～前面　　*go after* 走在～後面

72. Cheers!

Dialogue 1

A : I'm really happy that you could join me here for cocktails.
我真高興你能跟我一起來這兒參加雞尾酒會。

B : Well, it's been so long since we've done this together.
嗯，離我們上次一起參加酒會已經很久了。

A : I know. It has been a long time.
我知道。那是一段很長的時間。

B : Well, anyway, here's to our friendship.
噢，不管如何，這杯為我們的友誼。

A : To you and me. 為你和我。

B : Cheers! 乾杯！

Dialogue 2

A : John, why don't you join us for a drink?
約翰，你為何不加入我們喝杯酒？

B : Thanks. I will.
謝了，我會的。

A : Congratulations on your promotion.
恭喜你升官了。

B : Thank you. I'm really pleased about it.
謝謝你。我的確很高興。

A : You should be. Here's to your new job!
你應該的。這一杯祝你的新工作！

B : And here's to my good friends and fellow workers.
這一杯祝我的好友和工作夥伴們。

Dialogue 3

A : You're going to miss your sister now that she's married, aren't you?
　你姊姊結婚了，你將想念她，不是嗎？

B : I sure am. She made a lovely bride, didn't she?
　的確是。她是個可愛的新娘，不是嗎？

A : She was beautiful.
　她很漂亮。

B : This whole wedding has been splendid.
　這整個婚禮華麗而隆重。

A : Oh, look! They're about to toast the newlyweds.
　噢，看！他們正要去舉杯祝賀這對新婚夫婦。

B : Let's join them.
　我們加入他們吧。

〔舉一反三〕

A : I propose a toast to our first year in business.
　我提議舉杯祝頌咱們事業的第一年。

B : Cheers!
　乾杯！

A : It's Greg's birthday.
　這是葛瑞格的生日。

B : Congratulations, Greg. To your health.
　恭喜你，葛瑞格，祝你健康。

A : We make a great tennis team.
　我們組成一個偉大的網球隊。

B : I'll drink to that!
　我要為這喝一杯！

A : What shall we drink to?
　　　我們要為什麼而喝一杯？

B : I'll drink to you.
　　　我要為你喝一杯。

A : I propose a toast to our new partnership.
　　　我提議舉杯祝頌我們新的合作。

B : To our partnership's——"continued success."
　　　祝我們合作「不斷的成功」。

《 背景說明 》

　　　表示「乾杯！」有下列用法：*Cheers!* 或 *Bottoms up!* 此時祝賀的對象可能是個人或雙方全體，視前後文意而定。

　　　如果要表示對某人的祝賀，則可用：*To your health!*（祝你健康！）*To your success!*（祝你成功！）*Here's to Jim!*（祝福吉姆！）等。

【註釋】

cocktail（'kɑk,tel）n. 雞尾酒

cheer（tʃɪr）vi. 喝采歡呼　vt. 令人愉悅

drink 通常沒有特別指明何種飲料時，即指酒。

promotion（prə'moʃən）n. 晉陞；升遷

fellow workers 工作夥伴

bride（braɪd）n. 新娘　　bridegroom（'braɪd,grum）n. 新郎

splendid（'splɛndɪd）adj. 華麗的；堂皇的

toast（tost）vi. 舉杯祝頌；為（某人）乾杯

newlyweds（'njulɪ,wɛdz）n. pl. 新婚夫婦

partnership（'pɑrtnə,ʃɪp）n. 合夥；協力合作

73. *Don't beat around the bush*.

Dialogue 1

A : How much are you asking for this car?
這輛車你要賣多少錢？

B : You know, it's in great shape with new tires and a new paint job.
你知道，它有新輪胎，新噴漆，車型很棒。

A : Well, that sounds good but how much do you want for the car?
嗯，好像不錯，但是你這輛車要賣多少錢呢？

B : I forgot to mention the low mileage, too.
我忘記提到它的哩數也很低。

A : Don't beat around the bush! Tell me how much you want.
別拐彎抹角！告訴我你到底要多少錢。

B : Let's see, I'm sure we can come up with a fair price.
咱們看看，我確信我們可以談出個公平合理的價錢。

Dialogue 2

A : Mr. Chen, may I speak to you for a minute?
陳先生，我能跟你談一會兒嗎？

B : Yes. What do you want?
可以的。你要什麼？

A : I have a problem. I'd like to talk to you.
我有個問題。我想要跟你談談。

B : What is it?
是什麼？

A : Well, I don't really know how to say this....
嗯，我真不知道該怎麼說…。

B : Stop beating around the bush, get to the point.
別再拐彎抹角了，快說出重點。

Dialogue 3

A : Mr. Jones, are we going to work a full day on Saturday?
瓊斯先生，星期六我們將工作一整天嗎？

B : As far as I know, yes.
就目前我所知道，是的。

A : Is there any possibility that we'll work only half the day?
有沒有可能我們只工作半天？

B : I don't think so. Why?
我認為沒有。幹嘛？

A : I had hoped to go to my hometown this weekend.
我本來希望這個週末回家鄉去看看。

B : Don't beat around the bush, what do you want?
別拐彎抹角了，你要什麼？

〔舉一反三〕

A : Don't beat around the bush. Get to the point.
別再拐彎抹角，說出主題吧。

B : All right. 好的。

A : Did you want to ask me something?
你是不是要問我一些事啊？

B : Yes. I'll get right to the point.
是的。我會直接說出要點的。

A : What did he want? 他要什麼?
B : I don't know. He always beats around the bush.
　　我不知道。他總是拐彎抹角的。

A : Get to the point. 直接說出重點。
B : Mr. Brown, I'd like to marry your daughter.
　　布朗先生,我要娶你的女兒。

A : What was that phone call about?
　　那通電話是關於什麼的?
B : I don't know. He never got down to business.
　　我不知道。他一直沒有談到正題。

《背景說明》

　　beat around the bush 是指說話不明白坦率,儘是扯些無關痛癢的話,或是聲東擊西,吞吞吐吐。

　　譬如太太想要買委託行裡的流行套裝,但是價錢不低,不敢直接向先生開口,就扯了一些其他的話,如:「我衣櫥裡的衣服都太小了,而且都是舊款式的,根本不適合出門穿。」或「某某太太前天穿的那套衣服真漂亮,你覺得怎樣?」甚至對先生說:「你很久沒有添購新衣服了,我們去委託行逛一逛,看看有沒有合適的,好不好?」這就是 *beat around the bush* 「拐彎抹角」。

　　像上面這類情形,倒可以將計就計,故做糊塗,不必說:*Don't beat around the bush.* 以免破費。

【註釋】

in great shape 狀況很棒　　mileage〔'maɪlɪdʒ〕n. 哩程;哩數
beat around the bush 拐彎抹角
come up with 建議,此處指談出價錢。　　fair〔fɛr〕adj. 公正的;應當的
get to the point 直接切中主題;說出主題(重點)
as far as I know 就我所知道的

74. Push five, please.

Dialogue 1

A : Well, hello Lisa.

喲，哈囉，麗莎。

B : Hi, Jim.

嗨，吉姆。

A : I didn't know you worked here. What floor do you want?

我不知道妳在這兒工作。妳要到哪一樓？

B : Push five, please. I've been working here for almost a year.

請按五樓。我在這兒工作已經快一年了。

A : What company are you with?

妳在哪家公司工作？

B : Wang, Min and Wu. It's a law firm.

王明武，它是個律師事務所。

Dialogue 2

A : Let me help you with your packages.

讓我來幫你提行李。

B : I have them. Thank you, anyway.

我自己拿就可以。不管怎樣，謝謝你。

A : What floor do you want?

你要去幾樓？

B : Ten, please.

十樓。謝謝你。

A : Are you sure I can't help you?
　　你確定不需要我幫忙？

B : I'm okay, thank you.
　　我沒問題，謝謝你。

Dialogue 3

A : Hold it, please.
　　請等一下。

B : We just missed it.
　　我們剛錯過它。

A : It looked pretty full. Maybe the next one will be empty.
　　看起來相當擁擠。也許下一班會是空的。

B : Push the up button again.
　　再按一次上樓的鈕。

A : Do you work in this building?
　　你在這棟建築裏工作嗎？

B : Yes, on the fifth floor.
　　是的，在五樓。

〔舉一反三〕

A : What floor do you want?
　　你要到哪一樓？

B : Push five, please.
　　請按五樓。

A : Would you push seven, please?
　　請你按七樓好嗎？

B : I already have.
　　我已經按了。

A : Is this your floor?

這是你要到的那一樓嗎？

B : Yes. Excuse me, please.

是的。請借過。

A : Do you want off?

你要出去嗎？

B : Yes, this is my floor.

是的，這是我那一樓。

A : This is my floor. Out, please.

這是我要到的樓。請讓我出去。

B : I'm getting off, too.

我也正要出去。

【註釋】

law firm 法律事務所

package (ˈpækɪdʒ) *n.* 包裹；行李

hold (hold) *vt.* 保持～狀態

button (ˈbʌtn̩) *n.* 按鈕；鍵

75. *It's up in the air.*

Dialogue 1

A : I'm sorry but boarding has not yet started.
我很抱歉還沒有開始上船。

B : What seems to be the problem?
大概是什麼問題呢？

A : There's a mechanical problem.
有個機件上的問題。

B : When do you expect to start boarding?
你預期能在什麼時候開始上船？

A : It's up in the air. It might take twenty minutes or even longer.
尚未確定。可能要二十分鐘或者更久。

B : Will you announce when you're ready?
當你們準備好時，請你宣佈一下好嗎？

Dialogue 2

A : Are you going to the United States next week?
你下禮拜將去美國嗎？

B : No. The plans have been changed.
不，計畫已經改了。

A : I thought it was all set. 我以爲一切都定好了。

B : So did I, but something came up.
我原也以爲這樣，但是發生了一些事情。

A : Any idea of when you'll be going?
知不知道你何時會去？

B : No. Everything's up in the air.
不知道。一切都沒確定。

Dialogue 3

A : I heard you and your family were going to Tainan.
我聽說你和你家人要去台南。

B : We hope to.
我們希望去。

A : When are you going?
你們什麼時候去?

B : We don't know. Our plans are all up in the air.
不知道,我們的計畫都尚未確定。

A : Why?
為什麼?

B : The weather's been bad. We haven't been able to
get a flight.
天氣一直不好。我們沒有辦法搭乘飛機。

〔舉一反三〕

A : Are you leaving tomorrow?
你明天要離開了嗎?

B : No. My plans are still up in the air.
不。我的計畫仍然沒有確定。

A : Has Mike gotten that job yet?
麥克得到了那份工作嗎?

B : No. It's still up in the air.
不。仍然尚未確定。

A : Did Steve sign the contract?
史蒂夫簽了這份合約嗎?

B : No. He hasn't made a decision on it yet.
不。他還未做決定。

A : I thought your plans for winter vacation were all set.
　　我以爲你的寒假計畫都定好了。

B : They were, but now they're up in the air.
　　本來是的，但現在都無法確定。

A : Do you know when you're going to the United States?
　　你知道你何時要去美國嗎？

B : No. My plans aren't definite yet.
　　不。我的計畫尙未確定。

《背景說明》

　　這裡的 *It's up in the air.* 是指事情或計畫「尙未確定」（ un-decided ）。碰到別人問你：When do you plan to go to the States? 或 When do you get your promotion?如果還不確定，就說：*It's up in the air.*

　　此外 be up in the air 也可做「生氣」解，如 *He is up in the air.*（他在生氣。）還有幾個類似的成語：in the air「謠傳的；未確定的；在空中」；on the air「廣播中」，須注意不可混淆。

【註釋】

boarding〔'bordɪŋ〕n. 上船（或火車）
mechanical〔mə'kænɪkl̩〕adj. 機械上的　　　*up in the air* 未確定
announce〔ə'naʊns〕vt. 正式宣告；發表
all set 一切準備就緒；安排安當
come up 發生　　sign〔saɪn〕vt. 簽字
contract〔'kɑntrækt〕n. 合約；合同
definite〔'dɛfənɪt〕adj. 明確的；一定的

76. *Math is beyond me*.

Dialogue 1

A : Hi, Bill. How are you doing?
　　嗨，比爾。近況如何？

B : Pretty good. Yourself?
　　相當不錯。你呢？

A : Couldn't be better. How do you like your classes?
　　再好不過了。你喜歡你的課程嗎？

B : I like everything except math. Math is beyond me.
　　除了數學我每樣都喜歡。我對數學無能為力。

A : I like math. It's my major.
　　我喜歡數學。它是我的主修科目。

B : Would you help me then?
　　那麼請你幫我好嗎？

Dialogue 2

A : How long have you been in this country?
　　你在這國家多久了？

B : About three months.
　　大概三個月。

A : Is it hard for you to study at an American college?
　　對你來說，在美國大學裏求學是不是很困難？

B : Yes, I find it very difficult. Especially when you can't follow a professor's lecture.
　　是的，我發現非常困難。尤其是當你無法跟得上教授的講課時。

A : That's because you just arrived. Do you like biology?

那是因為你剛來。你喜歡生物學嗎？

B : No, it's beyond me.

不，我不懂。

Dialogue 3

A : Is that your son?

那是你兒子嗎？

B : Yes. He's home from school for the weekend.

是的。他從學校回來度周末。

A : What is he majoring in at college?

他在大學裏主修什麼？

B : Physics.

物理學。

A : Interesting. What area of physics?

很有趣。哪一範圍的物理學？

B : I really don't know. I don't understand half of what he says. It's beyond me.

我眞的不知道。他說的有一半我都不懂。我無能為力。

〔舉一反三〕

A : Do you like math?

你喜歡數學嗎？

B : No. It's beyond me.

不。無能為力。

A : Can you understand the current economic situation?

你了解現在的經濟情勢嗎？

B : No. It's beyond me.

不。我不懂。

A : Why is she quitting her job?

　　她爲何辭職？

B : I have no idea. Her reasoning is beyond me.

　　我毫無所知。她的理由我無法了解。

A : Do you have any notes from the lecture?

　　你有沒有這次演講的筆記？

B : No. I couldn't follow him. His theories are beyond
　　me.

　　沒有。我跟不上他。他的理論我不懂。

A : This computer is fantastic. It does everything.

　　這電腦眞奇妙。它什麼事都能做。

B : It's too complicated for me.

　　它對我來說太複雜了。

【註釋】

couldn't be better 再好也不過

math〔mæθ〕*n.* 數學（= mathematics〔͵mæθə'mætɪks〕）

beyond 爲～所不能及

major〔'medʒɚ〕*n.* 主修課程

lecture〔'lɛktʃɚ〕*n.* 演講（特指有教育和學術性者）；講課

biology〔baɪ'ɑlədʒɪ〕*n.* 生物學

physics〔'fɪzɪks〕*n.* 物理學

current〔'kɝənt〕*adj.* 現在的

quit〔kwɪt〕*vt.* 停止；辭去

notes 筆記

theory〔'θiərɪ〕*n.* 學說；理論

fantastic〔fæn'tæstɪk〕*adj.* 奇妙的

77. *Smoking or nonsmoking?*

Dialogue 1

A : May I see your ticket, please?
我能看看你的票嗎？

B : Here you are. 這是你要的。

A : Would you like a smoking or nonsmoking seat?
你要吸煙區或是非吸煙區的座位？

B : Nonsmoking, please.
非吸煙區的。

A : Window or aisle?
靠窗或是靠走道？

B : Window, please. 靠窗的。

Dialogue 2

A : I'm sorry, sir, I have no more window seats in the smoking section.
抱歉，先生，我沒有吸煙區靠窗的座位了。

B : Is there an aisle seat available?
靠走道的座位有沒有空的？

A : Yes. Do you want that?
有的，你要那位子嗎？

B : Is it in the rear of the plane?
它是在飛機的後部嗎？

A : No. It's over the wing.
不是。它在機翼那兒。

B : Fine. I'll take it.
很好。我就要它了。

Dialogue **3**

A : Where do you want to sit?

你想要坐哪兒?

B : In the nonsmoking section. Is that all right with you?

非吸煙區。對你沒有關係吧?

A : That's fine.

那很好。

B : You smoke though, don't you?

不過你抽煙,不是嗎?

A : Yes, but it's not a problem. I don't smoke that much.

是啊,但是那不成問題。我煙抽得沒有那麼凶。

B : Don't let me spoil your trip.

別讓我破壞了你的旅遊。

〔舉一反三〕

A : Do you want to sit in the smoking section?

你要坐在吸煙區裏嗎?

B : Yes, please. A window seat.

是的。請給我個靠窗的位子。

A : Extinguish your cigarette, please. No smoking during takeoff.

請熄滅香煙。起飛時禁止吸煙。

B : Would you open the ashtray, please?

請你打開煙灰盒好嗎?

A : What does that sign say?

那號誌說些什麼?

B : It says—No Smoking.

它說——禁止吸煙。

A : You can't smoke here.

　　你不能在這兒抽煙。

B : Why? There's no sign.

　　為何？沒有標誌說明。

A : Does this restaurant have a nonsmoking area?

　　這家餐廳有沒有非吸煙區？

B : Yes, over there.

　　有的，在那兒。

《背景説明》

　　買機票或車票時，售票員會問你 Would you like a seat in the *smoking or nonsmoking* section？如果對方忘了問你，最好自己主動告訴他：*Smoking, please.* 或 *Nonsmoking, please.* 免得上機或上車後造成不方便或不舒服。

　　這種分類制度在國外常常確實執行，不能抽煙的區域絕不可抽煙。國內近年來已有改善，但仍有些禁止吸煙的區域，出現癮君子吞雲吐霧，旁若無人。儘管如此，買票時還是説明自己的需要，既便己又利人。

　　與 Smoking or nonsmoking？類似的用法還有 *Window or aisle？*「靠窗或靠走道？」要用 *Window, please.* 或 *Aisle, please.* 回答。

【註釋】

nonsmoking〔nɑn'smokɪŋ〕*adj.* 不抽煙的　　aisle〔aɪl〕*n.* 走道

smoking section 吸煙區　　*nonsmoking section* 非吸煙區

available〔ə'veləbḷ〕*adj.* 可獲得的；有效的

rear〔rɪr〕*n.* 後半部；背部　　wing〔wɪŋ〕*n.* 機翼

spoil〔spɔɪl〕*vt.* 損傷；破壞　　extinguish〔ɪk'stɪŋgwɪʃ〕*vt.* 熄滅

takeoff〔'tek,ɔf〕*n.*（飛機）起飛　　ashtray〔'æʃ,tre〕*n.* 煙灰缸

78. *Would you do me a favor?*

Dialogue 1

A : Would you do me a favor?
   請幫我個忙好嗎?

B : Sure, if I can.
   當然,如果我能的話。

A : Could you get me a copy of Time magazine?
   你能不能幫我買一份時代雜誌?

B : No problem.
   沒問題。

A : The problem is I don't have any money.
   問題是我一點錢都沒有。

B : Well, then, that's your problem.
   噢,那麼,那是你的問題。

Dialogue 2

A : Why are you working late tonight?
   今晚你爲何工作得這麼晚?

B : I'm doing Dave a favor.
   我在幫戴夫一個忙。

A : Why? 爲什麼?

B : He had a date and wanted to leave early.
   他有個約會要早點離開。

A : How's he going to repay you?
   他將如何報答你?

B : I'm going to leave early tomorrow.
   我明天早點離開。

Dialogue 3

A : Are you leaving right now?

你現在就要離開了嗎?

B : Yes. Why?

是的。幹嘛?

A : Would you do something for me?

請為我做件事好嗎?

B : If I can. What do you want?

如果我能的話。你要什麼?

A : Would you drop my books off at the library on your way home?

請你在回家路上幫我把書還給圖書館好嗎?

B : Sure. I'd be glad to.

當然。我很樂意。

〔舉一反三〕

A : Would you do me a favor?

請你幫我個忙好嗎?

B : Sure. What do you want?

當然。你要什麼?

A : Why are you typing Bob's report?

你為什麼在打鮑伯的報告?

B : I'm doing him a favor.

我在幫他的忙。

A : Would you do something for me?

請你幫我做件事好嗎?

B : Sorry, I can't right now. I'm busy.

抱歉,我現在不能。我很忙。

A : Why did you call me?
　　你爲什麼打電話給我？

B : I wanted to ask you a favor.
　　我想請你幫個忙。

A : Could I ask you a favor?
　　我能請你幫個忙嗎？

B : Sure. What is it?
　　當然。是什麼呢？

【註釋】

do sb. a favor 幫某人的忙

copy〔'kɑpɪ〕*n.*（書籍、雜誌等的）冊；分

repay〔rɪ'pe〕*vt.* 報答；回報

drop ~ off 交付；遞送~

79. *I have to watch my weight.*

Dialogue 1

A : Did you order your lunch already?
你已經點好你的午餐嗎?

B : Yes. I'm having a salad.
是的,我要了一份沙拉。

A : Is that all you're having?
那就是你全部要的嗎?

B : Yes. I'm on a diet.
是的,我正在節食。

A : Why? 爲什麼?

B : I have to watch my weight.
我必須注意我的體重。

Dialogue 2

A : Would you like to drop by our place this evening for dessert?
今晚你要不要到我們這兒吃點心?

B : Oh, I'd like to, but I'm watching my weight.
噢,我想去,但是我正在注意我的體重。

A : That's all right. Come for a cup of coffee.
沒關係。來喝杯咖啡。

B : Well, O.K., maybe I will.
嗯,好吧,也許我會去。

A : Then it's settled, we'll see you about seven this evening. 那麼說定了,我們今晚大約七點見。

B : I'll see you then. 到時見。

Dialogue 3

A : Would you care for some candy or cookies?
你要一些糖果或是餅乾？

B : They really look delicious, but I have to slim down.
它們看起來眞可口，但是我必須減肥。

A : Are you on a diet?
你在節食嗎？

B : Yes. I've put on a few pounds this winter.
是的。今年冬天我重了幾磅。

A : I know what you mean. I've been on a diet, too.
我知道你的意思，我也在節食。

B : I didn't know that.
我不知道。

〔舉一反三〕

A : Would you like some ice cream?
你要一些冰淇淋嗎？

B : No, thank you. I have to watch my weight.
不了，謝謝你。我必須注意我的體重。

A : Your friend didn't eat any lunch.
你的朋友不吃午餐。

B : She's watching her weight.
她正在注意她的體重。

A : Are you trying to lose weight?
你正試著減輕體重嗎？

B : Yes. I want to slim down.
是的。我想瘦下來。

A : Aren't you going to have some pie?
　　你不吃些派嗎？

B : No. I have to watch what I eat. I'm overweight.
　　不了，我必須注意我所吃的。我體重過重。

A : Do you want some sugar in your coffee?
　　你咖啡要不要加點糖？

B : No, thank you. I'm trying to lose weight.
　　不了，謝謝你。我正試著減輕體重。

【註釋】

order〔'ɔrdɚ〕 vt. 點菜　　on a diet 節食中

drop by 順道拜訪

dessert〔dɪ'zɜt〕 n. 餐後的甜點

settled〔'sɛtl̩d〕 adj. 決定的

care for 喜歡；想要　　slim down 減肥

put on 增加

80. Where was I?

Dialogue 1

A : Let's back up, where was I?
　　我們折過頭去，我講到哪兒了？

B : You were talking about your trip to South Africa.
　　你在講有關你的南非之行。

A : Oh, yes, now I remember.
　　喔，對了，這會兒我想起來了。

B : So, how many people went on that trip with you?
　　那麼，多少人跟你一塊兒去旅行？

A : Five. 五個。

B : I bet you had a great time.
　　我相信你一定玩得很快樂。

Dialogue 2

A : Oh, where was I?
　　噢，我講到哪兒了？

B : You were going to tell me about that new restaurant.
　　你正要告訴我有關那間新餐廳。

A : Oh, right. They have great sweet and sour pork there.
　　喔，對的。他們的糖醋排骨眞棒。

B : Do they have any western dishes?
　　他們有西餐嗎？

A : Yes, they do, but their specialty is Chinese.
　　是的，他們有，但是他們拿手的是中國菜。

B : I'll have to try it.
　　我一定要去嚐嚐。

Dialogue 3

A : What was I saying?
我剛剛在說些什麼？

B : You were telling me about your son.
你在告訴我有關你的兒子。

A : Oh, that's right. Well, he's going to graduate in March.
噢，沒錯。嗯，他將於三月畢業。

B : Does he have a job?
他有工作嗎？

A : No. He's going to go to graduate school.
沒有。他要去唸研究所。

B : That's great!
那很好！

〔舉一反三〕

A : Where was I?
我講到哪兒了？

B : You were explaining why you're late today.
你在解釋你今天為何遲到。

A : I'm sorry for the interruption. What was I saying?
我很抱歉中途打斷。我剛才說些什麼？

B : You were telling me about your trip.
你在告訴我你的旅行。

A : What were we talking about?
我們剛剛在說些什麼？

B : We were discussing the employment situation.
我們在討論就業狀況。

A : What was I talking about when that phone rang?
　　電話鈴響的時候我正講什麼？

B : You were telling me about your vacation plans.
　　你正在告訴我你的假期計畫。

A : Go on with your story.
　　繼續你的故事。

B : Where was I?
　　我講到哪兒了？

【註釋】

back up 折回
had a great time 過得很愉快
western dishes 西式餐點
specialty (ˈspɛʃəltɪ) *n.* 專長；特製品
graduate school 研究所
interruption (ˌɪntəˈrʌpʃən) *n.* 中斷；打岔
employment situation 就業狀況

Go on with your story.

Where was I?

Editorial Staff

- **編譯** / 張 齡

- **校訂** / 劉 毅・謝靜芳・吳凱琳・蔡琇瑩・高瑋謙

- **校閱** / David Lightle・Bruce S. Stewart

- **封面設計** / 張鳳儀

- **美編** / 張鳳儀・蕭寶雲

- **打字** / 黃淑貞・吳秋香・蘇淑玲

||||||||||||| ●學習出版公司門市部●|||||||||||||||

台北地區：台北市許昌街 10 號 2 樓 TEL：(02)2331-4060・2331-9209
台中地區：台中市綠川東街 32 號 8 樓 23 室
　　　　　TEL：(04)223-2838

|||||||||||||||||||||||||||||||||||||||||||||||

五分鐘學會說英文 ②

編　　譯 / 張　齡

發 行 所 / 學習出版有限公司　　　　　☎ (02) 2704-5525

郵 撥 帳 號 / 0512727-2 學習出版社帳戶

登 記 證 / 局版台業 2179 號

印 刷 所 / 裕強彩色印刷有限公司

台 北 門 市 / 台北市許昌街 10 號 2 Ｆ　　　☎ (02) 2331-4060・2331-9209

台 中 門 市 / 台中市綠川東街 32 號 8 Ｆ 23 室　☎ (04) 223-2838

台灣總經銷 / 紅螞蟻圖書有限公司　　　☎ (02) 2799-9490・2657-0132

美國總經銷 / Evergreen Book Store　　☎ (818) 2813622

售價：新台幣一百八十元正

2000 年 2 月 1 日二版一刷